Robert Williams Buchanan

The wandering Jew

A Christmas carol by Robert Buchanan

Robert Williams Buchanan

The wandering Jew
A Christmas carol by Robert Buchanan

ISBN/EAN: 9783743306196

Manufactured in Europe, USA, Canada, Australia, Japa

Cover: Foto ©Andreas Hilbeck / pixelio.de

Manufactured and distributed by brebook publishing software
(www.brebook.com)

Robert Williams Buchanan

The wandering Jew

THE WANDERING JEW

A Christmas Carol

BY

ROBERT BUCHANAN

'*Quo diversus abis?*'

The oldest man he seemed that ever wore gray hairs!'

WORDSWORTH

London

CHATTO & WINDUS, PICCADILLY

1893

PRINTED BY

SPOTTISWOODE AND CO., NEW-STREET SQUARE

LONDON

TO MY DEAR FATHER

ROBERT BUCHANAN

POET AND SOCIAL MISSIONARY

THIS CHRISTMAS GIFT

Christmas 1892

Father on Earth, for whom I wept bereaven,
Father more dear than any Father in Heaven,
Flesh of my flesh, heart of this heart of mine,
Still quick, though dead, in me, true son of thine,
I draw the gravecloth from thy dear dead face,
I kiss thee gently sleeping, while I place
This wreath of Song upon thy holy head.

For since I live, I know thou art quick not dead,
And since thou art quick, yet drawest no living breath,
I know, dear Father, that there is Life in Death.

This, too, my Soul hath found--that if there were
No hope in Heaven, the world might well despair,
That thro' the mystery of my hope and love

I reach the Mystery that dwells above . . .

Father on Earth, still lying calm and blest

After long years of trouble and sad unrest,

Sleep,—while the Christ I paint for men to see

Seeketh the Fatherhood I found in thee !

THE WANDERING JEW

Errata

Page 5, line 3, *for* blew *read* flew
,,   41, line 5, *insert comma after* stood below

I reach the Mystery that dwells above . . .

Father on Earth, still lying calm and blest

After long years of trouble and sad unrest,

Sleep,—while the Christ I paint for men to see

Seeketh the Fatherhood I found in thee!

IE WANDERING JEW

Come, Faith, with eyes of patient heavenward gaze!

Come, Hope, with feet that bleed from thorny ways!

With hand for each, leading those twain to me,

Come with thy gifts of grace, fair Charity!

Bring Music too, whose voices trouble so

Our very footfalls as we graveward go,

Whose bright eyes, as she sings to Humankind,

Shine with the glory of God which keeps them blind!

Not to Parnassus, nor the Fabled Fount,

Nor to the folds of that Diviner Mount

Whereon our Milton kneeling prayed so deep,—

But hither, to this City stretched asleep

In silence, to this City of souls bereaven,

I call you, last hierophants of Heaven!

Come, Muses of the bleeding heart of Man,

Fairer than all the Nine Parnassian,

Fairer and clad in grace more heavenly

Than those sweet visions of Man's infancy,

Come from your lonely heights with song and prayer

To inspire an epos of the World's despair!

For lo, to that White Light which floweth from Him

Before whose gaze all sense and sight grow dim,

Holpen by you, his Angels pure and strong,

With tears I raise this tremulous Prism of Song!

O shine thereon, White Light, and melted be

Into the hues that lose themselves in Thee,

And tho' they are broken and but faintly show

Hints of the ray no sight may see or know,

On the poor Song let some dim gleam remain

To prove that Light Divine is never sought in vain!

I

As in the City's streets I.wander'd late,

Bitter with God because my wrongs seem'd great,

Chiller at heart than the bleak winds that blew

Under the star-strewn voids of steel-bright blue,

Sick at the silence of the Snow, and dead

To the white Earth beneath and Heaven o'erhead,

I heard a voice sound feebly at my side

In hollow human accents, and it cried

' For God's sake, mortal, let me lean on thee ! '

And as I turn'd in mute amaze to see

Who spake, there flew a whirlwind overhead

In which the lights of Heaven were darkenèd,

Shut out from sight or flickering sick and low

Like street-lamps when a sudden blast doth blow ;

But I could hear a rustling robe wind-swept

And a faint breathing; then a thin hand crept
Into mine own, clammy and cold as clay!

'Twas on that Night which ushereth in Christ's Day.
The winds had winnowèd the drifts of cloud,
But the white fall had ceased. There, pale and proud,
In streets of stone empty of life, while Sleep
In silvern mist hung beautiful and deep
Over the silent City even as breath,
I mused on God and Man, on Life and Death,
And mine own woe was as a glass wherein
I mirror'd God's injustice and Man's sin.
And so, remembering the time, I sneer'd
To think the mockery of Christ's birth-tide near'd,
And pitying thought of all the blinded herd
Who eat the dust and ashes of the Word,
Holding for all their light and all their good
The Woeful Man upon the Cross of wood;
And bitterly to mine own heart I said,
' In vain, in vain, upon that Cross he bled!

In vain he swore to vanquish Death, in vain

He spake of that glad Realm where he should reign !

Lo, all his promise is a foolish thing,

Flowers gathered by a child and withering

In the moist hand that holdeth them ; for lo !

Winter hath come, and on his grave the snow

Lies mountain-deep ; and where he sleeping lies

We too shall follow soon and close our eyes

Unvex'd by dreams.   The golden Dream is o'er,

And he whom Death hath conquer'd wakes no more ! '

Even then I heard the desolate voice intone,

And the thin hand crept trembling in my own,

And while my heart shut sharp in sudden dread

Against the rushing blood, I murmurèd

' Who speaks ? who speaks ? '   Suddenly in the sky

The Moon, a luminous white Moth, flew by,

And from her wings silent and mystical

Thick rays of vitreous dust began to fall,

Illuming Earth and Heaven ; when I was 'ware

Of One with reverend silver beard and hair

Snow-white and sorrowful, looming suddenly

In the new light like to a leafless Tree

Hung round with ice and magnified by mist

Against a frosty Heaven !   But ere I wist

Darkness return'd, the splendour died away,

And all I felt was that thin hand which lay

Fluttering in mine !

                Then suddenly again

I heard the tremulous voice cry out in pain

' For God's sake, mortal, let me lean on thee ! '

And peering thro' the dimness I could see

Snows of white hair blowing feebly in the wind ;

And deeply was I troubled in my mind

To see so ancient and so weak a Wight

At the cold mercy of the storm that night,

And said, while 'neath his wintry load he bent,

' Lean on me, father ! ' adding, as he leant

Feebly upon me, wearied out with woe,

' Whence dost thou come ? and whither dost thou go ? '

O then, meseem'd, the womb of Heaven afar

Quickened to sudden life, and moon and star

Flash'd like the opening of a million eyes,

Dimming from every labyrinth of the skies

Their lustre on that Lonely Man; and he

Loom'd like a comer from a far Countrie

In ragged antique raiment, and around

His waist a rotting rope was loosely bound,

And in one feeble hand a lanthorn quaint

Hung lax and trembling, and the light was faint

Within it unto dying, tho' it threw

Upon the snows beneath him light enew

To show his feeble feet were bloody and bare !

Thereon, with deep-drawn breath and dull dumb stare,

' Far have I travelled and the night is cold,'

He murmur'd, adding feebly, ' I am old ! '

He spake like one whose wits are wandering,

And strange his accents were, and seem'd to bring

The sense of some strange region far away ;

And like a cagèd Lion gaunt and grey

Who, looking thro' the bars, all woe-begone,

Beholdeth not the men he looketh on,

But gazeth thro' them on some lonely pool

Far in the desert, whither he crept to cool

His sunburnt loins and drink when strong and free,

Ev'n so with dull dumb stare he gazed thro' me

On some far bourne; and tho' his eyes were bright

They seem'd to suffer from the piteous light

They shed upon me thro' his hoary hair!

Then was I seized with wonder unaware

To see a man so old and strangely dight

Wandering alone beneath the Heavens that night;

For round us were the silenced haunts of trade,

The public marts and buildings deep in shade,

All emptied of their living waters; cold

And swift the stars did plunge thro' fold on fold

Of vaporous gauze, wind-driven; and the street

Was washen everywhere around my feet

With smoky silver; and the stillness round

Was dreadfuller by memory of the sound

Which fill'd the place all day from dawn to dark;

And strange it was and pitiful to mark

The heavy snow of years upon this Man,

His furrow'd cheeks down which the rheum-drops ran,

His wintry eyes that saw some summer land

Far off and very peaceful, while his hand

Dank as the drownèd dead's lay loose in mine.

But, my fear lessening, eager to divine

What man he was, and thro' what cruel fate

He wander'd homeless and disconsolate,

Scourged by the pitiless God who hateth men,

A victim, the more piteous in his pain

Because that God had given him length of days,

I cried, ' Who art thou ?   From what weary ways

Comest thou, father ?   Thou art frail and old !

Sad is thy lot upon a night so cold

To wander barefoot in a world of snow !

Speak to me, father ! for I fain would know
What cruel Hand is on thee out of Heaven,
That by the wintry tempests thou art driven
Hither and thither ?   Speak thy grief out strong,
For God, I know, is hard, and I, too, have my wrong

Then as I looked full eagerly on him,
And my limbs trembled, and mine eyes grew dim,
With dull still gaze he starèd on thro' me
At that far bourne of rest his Soul could see,
And shiver'd as the frost took blood and bone,
And even as a feeble child might moan
He murmurèd, ' I am hungry and athirst ! '

O then my soul was sicken'd, and I curst
The winds and snows that smote this Man so old,
And drave him outcast thro' the wintry wold,
And made the belly of him tight with pain
For lack of food, and only with the rain
Moisten'd his toothless gums ! and 'neath my breath

I curst the pitiless Lord of Life and Death,

And ' all the hate I bare for Him who wrought

This crumbling prison-house of flesh (methought)

Is vindicated by this Wight who bears

The rueful justification of grey hairs ! '

And as I held his clay-cold hand, nor spake,

For I was hoarse with sorrow for his sake,

He cried in a strange, witless, wandering way,

Not loud, but as a burthen children say

When they have known it long by heart, ' Aye me !

The blessèd Night is dark on land and sea,

On tired eyes the dusts of Sleep are shed,

And yet I have no place to rest my head ! '

Ev'n as he spake there flash'd across my sight

A glamour of the Sleepers of the Night :

The hushèd rooms where dainty ladies dream,

And shaded night-lamps shed a slumberous gleam

Across the silken sheets and broider'd couch ;

The beggarman, a groat within his pouch,

Pillow'd on filthy rags and chuckling deep

Because his dreams are golden; the sweet sleep

Of little children holding in pink palm

The fancied toy, and smiling; slumbers calm

Of delicate-limb'd vestals, slumbers wild

Of puerperal women and of nymphs defiled

Wasting like rotten fruit;—as scenes we see

By lightning flashes, changing momently,

These visions came and went, each gleaming clear

Yet spectral, in the act to disappear;

I mark'd the long streets empty to the sky,

And every dim square window was an eye

That gazing dimly inward saw within

Some hidden mystery of shame or sin,—

Lovebed and deathbed, raggedness and wealth,

Pale Murder, tiptoe, creeping on in stealth

With sharp uplifted knife, or haggard Lust

Mouthing his stolen fruit of tasteless dust;

And then I saw strange huddled shapes that lay

In blankets under palm trees, while the day

Drew far across the sands its bloodred line;
The sailor drearily dozing, while the brine
Flash'd eyes of foam around him; glimpses then
Of purple royal chambers, where pale men
Lay naked of their glory; and of the warm
Bonfires on mountain sides, where many a form
Lay prone but gript the sword; of halls of stone
Lofty and cold, where wounded men made moan,
And the calm nurse stole softly down the row
Of narrow sickbeds, like a ghost; and lo!
These pictures swiftly came and vanishèd
Like northern meteors, leaving as they fled
A trouble like the wash of leaden seas.

Then, while the glamour of such images
Weighed on my Soul, I said, ' Hard by I dwell,—
Poor is the place, yet thou mayst find it well
After thy travail. Thither let us go! '
And by my side he falter'd feeble and slow,
Breathing the frosty air with pain, and soon

We reached a lonely Bridge o'er which the Moon

Hung phosphorescent, blinding with its wings

The lamps that flicker'd there like elfin things ;

But near us, on the water's brim, engloom'd

In its own night, a mighty Abbey loom'd,

Clothen with rayless snow as with a shroud ;

And suddenly that old Man cried aloud,

Lifting his weary face and woe-begone

Up to the painted windowpanes that shone

With frosty glimmers, 'Open, O thou Priest

Who waitest in the Temple ! '   As he ceased,

The fretted arches echoed to the cry

And with a shriek the wintry wind went by

And died in silence.   For a moment's space

He stood and listened with upturnèd face,

Then moan'd and faltered on in dumb despair,

Until we stood upon the Bridge, and there

The vitreous light was luminously drawn,

Making the lamps burn dim, as in a ghostly dawn.

II

Vaster and mightier a thousandfold
Than Babylon or Nineveh of old,
Shrouded in snow the silent City slept;
And through its heart the great black River crept
Snakewise, with sullen coils that as they wound
Flash'd scales of filmy silver; all around
The ominous buildings huddled from the light
With cold grey roofs and gables tipt with white,
And lines of lamps made a pale aqueous glow
With streaks of crimson in the pools below
Between the clustering masts. 'Twas still, like Death!
Still as a snow-clad grave! No stir! No breath!
A mist of silence o'er the City asleep,
A frozen smoke of incense that did creep
From Life's deserted Altar. And on high

C

Clouds white as wool that melted o'er the sky
Before the winnowing beams.   In Heaven's Serene
No sound! no stir! but all the still stars, green
With their exceeding lustre, shedding light
From verge to verge of the great dome of Night,
And scattering hoarfrost thro' the lustrous space
Between their spheres and the dark dwelling place
Of mortals blind to sight and dead to sound.

So lay the silent City glory-crowned,
All the rich blood of human life that flows
Thro' its dark veins hushèd in deep repose,
The pulses of its heart scarce felt to beat,
Calm as a corpse, the snow its winding sheet,
The sky its pall; and o'er its slumbers fell
The white Moon's luminous and hypnotic spell,
As when some bright Magician's hands are prest
With magic gloves upon a Monster's breast,
So that the heart just flutters, and the eyes
Shut drowsily!—But it dream'd beneath the skies

God knows what dreams! What dreams of Heavens
    unknown,
Where sits the Lord of Life on his white Throne,
While angel-wings flash thick as fowl that flee
Round islands Hebridean, when the Sea
Burns to a molten sapphire of dead calm!

Upon my fever'd eyes fell soft as balm
The ablution of the Midnight, as once more
I led that old Man weary and footsore,
Guiding his steps, while ever and anon
He paused in pain ; and thro' the light that shone
O'er the still Bridge we falter'd, with no sound.

Then, as he paused for breath, and gazed around,
Again I questioned gently whence he came,
His place of birth, his kindred, and his name,
And whisper'd softly, ' I can surely see
Thou art a comer from a far Countrie,
And thou art very old!'—'So old! so old!'

He answered, shivering in the moonlight cold ;
Then raised his head, upgazing thro' the Night,
And threw his arms up quick, and rose his height,
Crying, ' For ever at the door of Death
Faintly I knock, and when it openeth
Would fain creep in, but ever a Hand snow-cold
Thrusteth me back into the open wold,
And ever a voice intones early and late
" Until thy work is done, remain and wait ! "
And century after century I have trod
The infinitely weary glooms of God,
And lo ! the Winter of mine age is here ! '

Even as he spake, in a low voice yet clear,
Clinging upon me, with his hungry eyes
Cast upward at the cold and pitiless skies,
His white hair blent with snows around him blown,
And his feet naked on the Bridge of stone,
Methought I knew that Wanderer whom God's curse
Scourgeth for ever thro' the Universe

Because he mocked with words of blasphemy

God's Martyr on the path to Calvary,

Yea, did deny him on his day of Death !

Wherefore, with shuddering sense and bated breath

I gazed upon him.   Shivering he stood there,

The consecration of a vast despair

Cast round him like a raiment ; and ere I knew

I moaned aloud, ' Thou art that Wandering Jew

Whose name all men and women know too well ! '

Strangely on me his eyes of sorrow fell,

And bending low, as doth a wind-blown tree,

In a low voice he answer'd :

> ' I am He ! '

O NIGHT of wonder!   O enchanted Night!

Full of strange whisperings and wondrous ligh.

How shall I, singing, summon up again

Thine hours of awe and deep miraculous pain?

For as I stood upon those streets of stone

I seem'd to hear the wailing winds intone

'AHASUERUS!'—while with lips apart,

His thin hand prest upon his fluttering heart,

His face like marble lit by lightning's glare,

His frail feet bleeding, and his bosom bare,

List'ning he stood!

From the blue Void o'erhead

Starlight and moonlight round his shape were shed,

And the chill air was troubled all around

With piteous wails and echoes of such sound

As fills the great sad Sea on nights of Yule,

When all the cisterns of the heavens are full

And one great hush precedes the coming Storm.

And like a snow-wrapt statue seem'd the form

I looked on, and of more than mortal height!

Wintry his robe, his hair and beard snow-white

Frozen like icicles, his face all dim,

And in the sunken, sunless eyes of him

Silent despair, as of a lifeless stone!

And then meseem'd that in some frozen zone,

Where never flower doth blossom or grass is green,

Chill'd to the heart by cruel winds and keen

Shiv'ring I stood, and the thick choking breath

Of Frost was round me, terrible as Death,

And he I look'd on was a figure wan

Hewn out of snow in likeness of a Man;

And all the silent City in a trice

Was turn'd to domes and towers of rayless ice,

As of some spectral City whose pale spires

Are lighted dimly with the auroral fires
That gleam for ever at the sunless Pole!

How long this glamour clung upon my Soul
I know not; but at last methought I spake,
Like one who, fresh from vision, half awake,
Murmurs his thought—'Father of men that roam,
Outcast from God and exile from thy home,
(If such there be for any Soul in need)
I will not say, God bless thee, since indeed
God's blessing is a burthen and a blight;
Yet will I bless thee, in that God's despite,
Knowing thy sorrow manifold and deep.
Aye me, aye me, what may I do but weep,
Seeing thy poor grey hair, and frail shape driven
Hither and thither by the winds of Heaven,
Sharing thy sorrow, hearing thy sad moan
That penetrates all hearts but God's alone,
Knowing thee mortal, yet predoom'd to fare
For ever, with no restplace anywhere,

Although all other mortal things may die !

Death is the one good thing beneath the sky ;

Death is the one sweet thing that men may see ;

Yet even this God doth deny to thee !

Thou canst not die ! ' With feeble lips of clay

He answered, yet the voice seem'd far away,

' Yea, Death is best, and yet I cannot die ! '

Before my vision, as I heard the cry,

There flash'd a glamour of the Dead ; and lo !

I saw a hooded Phantom come and go

Across great solitary plains by night,

Red with all nameless horror of the fight,

And dead white faces glimmer'd from the sward,

And here a helmet gleamed and there a sword,

And all was still and dreadful, and the scent

Of carnage thickened where the Phantom went.

This faded, and methought I stood stone-still

In a great Graveyard strewn with moonbeams chill

Like bleaching shrouds, and through the grassy glooms

Pale crosses glimmer'd and great marble tombs;

But as I crost my frozen hands to pray

The apparition changed and died away,

And I was walking very silently

Some oozy bottom of the sunless Sea.

And midst the sombre foliage I could mark

Black skeletons of many a shipwreck'd bark

Within whose meshes, washing to and fro,

Were skeletons of men as white as snow

Picked clean by many a hideous ocean-thing.

The waters swung around me as they swing

Round drowning men, and with a choking pain

I struggled,—and that moment saw again

The sleeping City and the cold Moonshine,

And in the midst, with his blank eyes on mine,

That Man of Mystery who could not die!

And lo, his lips were openèd with a cry,

And his lean hands were stretchèd up to Heaven.

' Ah, woe is me,' he said, ' to stand bereaven

Of that which every man of clay may share!

Eternity hath snowed upon my hair,

And yet, though feeble and weary, I endure.

Still might I fare, if Death at last were sure,

If I might see, eternities away,

A grave, wide open, where my feet might stay ! '

Then in a lower voice more deep with dread,

' Father which art in Heaven,' the old Man said,

' Thou from the holy shelter of whose wing

I came, an innocent and shining thing,

A lily in my hand and in mine eyes

The passion and the peace of Paradise,

Thou who didst drop me gently down to rest

A little while upon my Mother's breast,

Wrapt in the raiment of a mortal birth,

How long, how long, across thy stricken Earth

Must I fare onward, deathless ?   Tell me, when

May *I* too taste the cup thou givest to men,

My brethren and thy children and the heirs

Of all my spirit's sorrows and despairs ?

My work is o'er—my sin (if sin there be)

Is buried with the bones of Calvary ;

My blessing has been spoken, and my curse

Is wingèd vengeance in thy Universe ;

My voice hath thrill'd thy dark Eternity

To protestation and to agony,

And Man hath listen'd with wild lips apart

As to a cry from his own breaking heart !

What then remains for me to do, O God,

But fold thin hands and bend beneath thy rod,

And ask for respite after labour done ? '

In sorrow and in awe he spake, as one

Communing with some Shape I could not mark,

And all his words seem'd wild, his meaning dark ;

And as he ceased the Heavens grew dark in woe,

And faster, thicker, fell the encircling Snow,

Wrapping him with its whiteness round and round ;

But from the Void above no sign, no sound,

Came answering his prayer.

       ' Father,' I said,

' Chill falls the snow upon thy holy head,

(Yea, holy through much sorrow 'tis to me)

And He to whom thou prayest so piteously

Hears not, and will not hear, and hath not heard

Since first the Spirit of Man drew breath and stirred !

Let us seek shelter ! ' But I spake in vain—

He heard not; but as one that dies in pain

Sank feebly on the parapet of stone.

Upon his naked breast the Snow was blown

Thicker and colder—on his hoary head

Heavily like a cruel hand of lead

It thickened—so he stood from head to feet

Smother'd and wrapt as in a winding sheet,

Forlorn and weary, panting, overpowered.

Then lo ! a miracle !—For a space he cowered

As if o'ermastered by the cruel touch,

But all at once, as one that suffers much

Yet quickeneth into anger suddenly,

He said, in a sharp voice of sovereignty,

' Cease, cease ! ' and at the very voice's sound,

The white Snow wildly wavering round and round

Rose like a curtain, leaving all things bright !

Spell-bound and wonder-stricken at the sight,

And comprehending not its import yet,

(For still my Soul with fever and with fret

Was laden, and I bore upon my mind

The darkness of that doubt that keeps men blind)

I cried, ' See ! see ! the elemental Snow

Obeys thy call, in pity for thy woe—

Gentler than He who fashioned men for pain,

The white Snow and the wild Wind and the Rain

Would bless thee, and there is no cruel beast

Which He·hath made, the greater or the least,

Which would not spare thy life and lick thy hand,

Poor outcast comer from a lonely land.

Yea, only God is cruel—Only He

Whose foot is on the Mountains and the Sea,

And on the bruisèd frame and flesh of Man ! '

IV

Lo, now the Moonlight lit his features wan

With spectral beams, and o'er his hoary hair

A halo of brightness fell, and rested there !

And while upon his face mine eyes were bent

In utterness of woeful wonderment,

Into mine ear the strange voice crept once more—

' Far have I wandered, weary and spirit-sore,

And lo ! wherever I have chanced to be,

All things, save men alone, have pitied me ! '

Then—then—even as he spake, forlornly crown'd

By the cold light that wrapt him round and round,

I saw upon his twain hands raised to Heaven

Stigmata bloody as of sharp nails driven

Thro' the soft palms of mortals crucified !

And swiftly glancing downward I descried
Stigmata bloody on the naked feet
Set feebly on the cold stones of the street !—
And moveless in the frosty light he stood,
Ev'n as one hanging on the Cross of wood !

Then, like a lone man in the north, to whom
The auroral lights on the world's edge assume
The likeness of his gods, I seem'd to swoon
To a sick horror ; and the stars and moon
Reel'd wildly o'er me, swift as sparks that blow
Out of a forge ; and the cold stones below
Chattered like teeth !   For lo, at last I knew
·The lineaments of that diviner Jew
Who like a Phantom passeth everywhere,
The World's last hope and bitterest despair,
Deathless, yet dead !—

                 Unto my knees I sank,
And with an eye glaz'd like the dying's drank
The wonder of that Presence !

　　　　　　　　　　　　White and tall

And awful grew He in the mystical

Chill air around Him,—at His mouth a mist

Made by His frosty breathing!—Then I kissed

His frozen raiment-hem, and murmurèd

'Adonai! Master! Lord of Quick and Dead!'

'Twas more than heart could suffer and still beat—

So with a hollow moan I fainted at his feet!

V

O YE, ye ancient men born yesterday,

Some few of whom may in this Yuletide lay

Feel echoes of your own hearts, listen on,

Till the faint music of the harp is gone

And the weak hand drops leaden down the string !

For lo, I voice to you a mystic thing

Whose darkness is as full of starry gleams

As is a tropic twilight; in your dreams

This thing shall haunt you, and become a sound

Of friendship in still places, and around

Your lives this thing shall deepen, and impart

A music to the trouble of the heart,

So that perchance, upon some gracious day,

Ye may bethink you of the Song, and pray

That God may bless the Singer for your sake !

Not unto bliss and peace did I awake

From that deep swoon, nor to the garish light

Wherein all spiritual things grow slight

And vanish—nay!—the midnight and the place

Had changèd not, and o'er me still the Face

Shone piteously serene; I felt its ray

On mine unclosèd eyelids as I lay;

Then gazing up, blinking mine eyes for dread

Of some new brightness, I discern'd instead

That Man Forlorn, and as I gazed he smiled

Even as a Father looking on a child!

Aye me! the sorrow of that smile! 'Twas such

As singer ne'er may sing or pencil touch!—

But ye who have seen the light that is in snow,

The glimmer on the heights where sad and slow

Some happy day is dying—ye who have seen

Strange dawns and moonlit waters, woodlands green

Troubled with their own beauty; think of these,

And of all other tender images,

Then think of some belovèd face asleep

'Mid the dark pathos of the grave, blend deep

Its beauty with all those until ye weep,

And ye may partly guess the woe divine

Wherewith that Face was looking down on mine,—

While trembling, wondering, like a captive thrown

By cruel hands into some cell of stone,

Who waiting Death to end his long despair

Sees the door open and a friend stand there

Bringing new light and life into his prison,

I faltered, ' Lord of Life, hast thou *arisen* ? '

' *Arisen ! Arisen ! Arisen !* '

At the word

The silent cisterns of the Night were stirred

And plash'd with troublous waters, and in the sky

The pale stars clung together, while the cry

Was wafted on the wind from street to street !

Like to a dreaming man whose heart doth beat

With thick pulsations, while he fights to break

The load of terror with a shriek and wake,

The sleeping City trembled thro' and thro';

And in its darkness, open'd to my view

As by enchantment, those who slumberèd

Rose from their pillows, listening in dread;

And out of soot-black windows faces white

Gleamed ghost-like, peering forth into the night;

And haggard women by the River dark,

Crawling to plunge and drown, stood still to heark;

And in the silent shrouded Hospitals,

Where the dim night-lamp flickering on the walls

Made woeful shadows, men who dying lay,

Picking the coverlit as they pass'd away

And babbling babe-like, raised their heads to hear,

While all their darkening sense again grew clear,

And moaned ' Arisen ! Arisen ! ' and in his cell

The Murderer, for whom the pitiless bell

Would toll at dawn, sat with uplifted hair

And broke to piteous impotence of prayer !

Then all grew troubled as a rainy Sea,

I sank in stupor, struggling to be free

Even as a drowning wight; and as the brain

Of him who drowneth flasheth with no pain

Into a sudden vision of things fled,

Faces forgotten, places vanishèd

Came, went, and came again, and 'mid it all

I knew myself the weary, querulous, small,

Weak, wayward Soul, with little hope or will,

Crying for ' God, God, God,' and thrusting still

Cain's offering on His altar.   All this past—

Then came a longer darkness—and at last

I found myself upon my feet once more

Tottering and faint and fearful, a dull roar

Of blood within mine ears, still crying aloud

' Arisen !   Arisen !   Arisen ! ' . . .

      Whereon the cloud

Of wonder lifted, and again mine eyes

Saw the sad City sleeping 'neath the skies,

Silent and flooded with the white Moon's beams

As still as any City seen in dreams ;

And lo! the great Bridge, and the River that ran

Blindly beneath it, and that hoary Man

Standing thereon with naked piercèd feet

Uplooking to the Heavens as if to meet

Some vision; and the abysses of the air

Had opened, and the Vision was shining there!

Far, far away, faint as a filmy cloud,

A Form Divine appeared, her bright head bowed,

Her eyes down-looking on a Babe she prest

In holy rapture to her gentle breast,

And tho' all else was ghost-like, strange, and dim,

A brightness touched the Babe and cover'd Him,—

Such brightness as we feel in summer days

When hawthorn blossoms scent the flowery ways

And all the happy clay is verdure-clad;

And the Babe seem'd as others who make glad

The homes of mortals, and the Mother's face

Was like a fountain in a sunny place

Giving and taking gladness, and her eyes

Beheld no other sight in earth or skies

Save the blest Babe on whom their light did shine;

But he, that little one, that Babe Divine,

Gazed down with reaching hands and face aglow

Upon the Lonely Man who stood below

And smiled upon him, radiant as the morn!

Whereat the weary Christ raised arms forlorn

And answer'd with a thin despairing moan!

And at the sound Darkness like dust was blown

Over the Heavens, and the sweet Vision fled,

And all that wonder of the night was dead! . . . .

Yet still I saw him looming woebegone

Upon the lonely Bridge, and faltering on

With feeble feet beneath the falling snow,

And in his hand the lamp hung, flickering low

As if to die, yet died not. Far away

He seemèd now, altho' so near,—a grey

Ghost seen in dreams; yet even as dreams appear

To one who sleeps more mystically clear

Than any vision of the waking sight,

He shone upon the sadness of the Night

As softly as a star, while all around

Loom'd the great City, sleeping with no sound

Save its own deep-drawn breath.   Yet I could
    mark

The glimmer of eyes that watched him from the
    dark

Shadows beyond the Bridge, and, where the rays

Of the dim moonlight lit the frozen ways,

Shapes crouching low or crawling serpent-wise

Waited to catch the pity of his eyes

Or touch his raiment-hem !

                            Then, while I wept

For pity of his loneliness, and crept

In wonder after him, with bated breath,

Fell a new Darkness deep and dread as Death ;

And from the Darkness came tumultuously

Clangour and roar as of a storm-torn Sea,—

And, shrill as shrieks of ocean-birds that fly
Over the angry waters, rose the cry
Of human voices!

    Then the four Winds blew
Their clarions, while the stormy tumult grew,
And all was dimly visible again.

VI

METHOUGHT I stood upon an open Plain
Beyond the City, and before my face
Rose, with mad surges thundering at its base,
A mountain like Golgotha ; and the waves
That surgèd round its sunless cliffs and caves
Were human—countless swarms of Quick and Dead !

Then, while the fire-flaught flickered overhead,
I saw the Phantoms of Golgotha throng
Around that ancient Man, who trailed along
A woeful Cross of Wood ; and as he went,
His body bruisèd and his raiment rent,
His bare feet bleeding and his force out-worn,
They pricked him on with spears and laughed in scorn,
Shouting, ' At last Thy Judgment Day hath come ! '

And when he faltered breathless, faint, and dumb,

And stumbled on his face amid the snows,

They dragged him up and drave him on with blows

To that black Mountain !

                      Then my soul was 'ware

Of One who silent sat in Judgment there

Shrouded and spectral; lonely as a cloud

He loomed above the surging and shrieking crowd.

Human he seemèd, and yet his eyeballs shone

From fleshless sockets of a Skeleton,

And from the shroud around him darkly roll'd

He pointed with a fleshless hand and cold

At those who came, and, in a voice that thrill'd

The tumult at his feet till it was still'd,

Cried :

       'Back, ye Waters of Humanity !

Wait and be silent.   Leave this Man to me.

The centuries of his weary watch have pass'd,

And lo ! the Judgment Time is ripe at last.

Stand up, thou Man whom men would doom to death,
And speak thy Name !'

'JESUS OF NAZARETH ! '
Answer'd the Man.

And as he spake his name,
The multitude with thunderous acclaim
Shriek'd !

But again the solemn voice, which thrill'd
The tumult and the wrath till they were still'd,
Cried :

' Peace, ye broken hearts, have patience yet !
This Man is surely here to pay his debt
To Death and Time.'

And to the Man he said :

' Jesus of Nazareth, lift up thy head
And hearken !   Brought to face Eternity
By men, thy brethren, form'd of flesh like thee,
Brought here by men to me, the Spirit of Man,

To answer for thy deeds since life began,

Brought hither to Golgotha, whereupon

Thyself wast crucified in days long gone,

Thou shalt be judged and hear thy judgment spoken

Before the World whose slumbers thou hast broken.

Thou saidst, "I have fought with Death and am the
    stronger !

Wake to Eternal Life and sleep no longer ! "

And men, thy brethren, troubled by thy crying,

Have rush'd from Death to seek the Life undying,

And men have anguish'd, wearied out with waiting

For the great unknown Father of thy creating,

And now for vengeance on thy head they gather,

Crying, " Death reigns ! There is no God—no Father! " '

He ceased, and Jesus spake not, but was mute

In woe supreme and pity absolute.

Then calmly amid the shadows of the Throne

Another awful shrouded Skeleton,

Human yet more than human, rose his height,

With baleful eyes of wild and wistful light,
And said :

       ' O Judge, Death reigned since Time began,
Sov'ran of Life and Change! and ere this Man
Came with his lying dreams to break our rest
The reign of Death was beautiful and blest!
But now within the flesh of men there grows
The poison of a Dream that slays repose,
The trouble of a mirage in the air
That turneth into terror and despair ;
So that the Master of the World, ev'n Death,
Hated in his own kingdom, travaileth
In darkness, creeping haunted and afraid,
Like any mortal thing, from shade to shade,
From tomb to tomb ; and ever where he flies
The seed of men shrink with averted eyes,
And call with mad yet unavailing woe
On this Man and his God to lay Death low.
Wherefore the Master of the Quick and Dead
Demandeth doom and justice on the head

Of Him, this Jew, who hath usurp'd the throne
The Lord of flesh claims ever for his own.

This Jew hath made the Earth that once was glad
A lazar-house of woeful man and mad
Who can yet will not sleep, and in their strife
For barren glory and eternal Life,
Have rent each other, murmuring his Name!'

He paused—and from the listening host there came
Tumult nor voice—there was no sound, no stir,
But all was hushèd as a death-chamber;
And while that pallid shrouded Skeleton
In a low voice like funeral bélls spake on,
From heart to heart a nameless horror ran.

E

VII

' In the name of all men I arraign this Man,

Named Jesus, son of Joseph, and self-styled

The Son of God!

      ' Born in the East, the child

Of Jewish parents, toiling for their bread,

He grew to manhood, following, it is said,

His father's humble trade of carpentry ;

But hearing one day, close to Galilee,

One John, a madman, in the desert crying,

Baptising all who came and prophesying,

This Jesus also long'd to prophesy ;

And lo ! ere very many days went by,

He left his tools, forsook his native town,

And for a season wandered up and down

On idle preaching bent. Now, as we know,

Madness and Falsehood wedded are, and grow

With what they breed ; so the Accused ere long,

Finding his audience fit, his rivals strong

(For prophets in those realms were thick as bees),

Began to invent such fables as might please

The ears of ignorant wonder-seeking men,

And finding 'mong the Jewish race just then

The wild old prophecy of a Christ and King,

Destined to lead the race, still lingering,

He threw the royal raiment ready made

On his bare back, and blasphemously played

The Christ they craved for !—next, to clinch his claim,

And prove his Godhead not an empty name,

The Man wrought miracles, calling to his aid

Simple devices of the wizard's trade,

Healing the sick—nay, even, 'twas avowed,

Bidding a dead man quicken in his shroud !

Pass over that as idle—turn with me

To the completion of his infamy !

In time, when he had sown with such false seed

Rank madness broadcast like an evil weed,

Choking the wholesome fields of industry,

And setting all the fiends of folly free,

This Jesus, with great numbers following,

Rides to Jerusalem like any King,

And thronèd on an ass goes thro' the Gate.

Arrived within the City, he keeps his state

With publicans and harlots, vaunts abroad

His proud vocation as the Son of God,

And last, presuming on his pride of place,

Profanes the Holy Temple of the race.

The rest we know—they slew him, as was right,

Set him upon a Cross in all men's sight,

Then, lastly, buried him.   And now 'twas thought

The Man had made amends; the ill he wrought

Died with him, since his foolish race was run.

Not so; the Man's black crime had scarce begun !

For on the Sabbath day, as scribes aver,

Three Women, watching by his Sepulchre,

Beheld the stone roll'd back, and in the gloom

Beyond, a cast-off shroud and empty tomb!

The Man had risen, and that very day

Appeared among the faithful far away,

Spake, vanish'd, and was never after seen

By those who knew him, loved him, and had been

His life-long followers.'   .

                Now, hear and heed—

Had this Man, like the rest of Adam's seed,

Rested within his grave, turned back to dust,

Accepted dissolution, as were just,

Well had it been for him and all man's race!

He rose, this Jew—but in what secret place

He for a season hid his evil head

We know not; followers of his tribe have said

He walked with bleeding feet dejectedly

The lava shores of Hell (if Hell there be!),

Pondering his plan to lead the world astray—

But after sundry years had past away

Mortals began to see in divers lands

A Phantom pale with piercèd feet and hands

Who cried, ' I am the Christ—believe on me—

Or lose your Souls alive eternally ! '

And of those men a few believed, and cried

' Lo ! Christ is God, and God we crucified !

But He shall come to judge the Quick and Dead ! '

Now, mark the issue.   Where this rumour spread,

All other gentle gods that gladden'd Man

Faded and fled away ; the priests of Pan,

That singing by Arcadian rivers rear'd

Their flowery altars, wept and disappeared ;

And men forgot the fields and the sweet light,

Joy, and all wonders of the day and night,

All splendours of the sense, all happy things,

Art, and the happy Muses' ministerings,

Forgot that radiant house of flesh divine

Wherein each Soul is shut as in a shrine,

Because this Phantom, like a shape in sleep,

Showing his red wounds, murmur'd, ' Pray! and weep!'

And when fair Earth, mother of things of clay,

The gladsome Mother, now grown gaunt and grey,

Cried to her children, ' Children, stay with me!

I made you happy, innocent, and free!

Although this Man, my latest born, your brother,

Casts dust in the living eyes of me, his mother,

Follow him not, forsake me not, but stay! '

They too, because He beckon'd, turned away,

Or cursing her who bare them, they too shed

Dust in her eyes, dishonour on her head.

First, in her name, the Mother of all our race,

Whom this unfilial hand smote in the face,

Whom he defamed and shamed with cheats and lies,

And taught a thousand children to despise,

I demand justice on her Son, this Jew!—

Pass on. The rumour of his godhead grew;

Yea, men were conscious of a Presence sad,

Crownèd with thorns, in ragged raiment clad,

Haunting the sunless places of the Earth ;

And mystic legends of his heavenly birth,

His many miracles, his piteous death,

Were whisper'd by the faithful underbreath ;

And wights grown sick from tearfullest despairs,

And many weary souls worn out with cares,

Sick men and witless, all who had assailed

The gleaming heights of Happiness and failed,

But chiefly women bruised and undertrod,

Believed this Man indeed the Son of God,—

Because he said, ' the high shall be estranged,

The low uplifted, and the weak avenged,

And blest be those who have cast this world away

To await the dawning of my Judgment Day ! '

And straightway many yielded up their lives,

Blasphemed their bodies, gash'd their flesh with knives,

In attestation that these things were true.

And I deny not that to some, a few

Poor Souls without a hope, without a friend,

The lie brought comfort and a peaceful end ;

Nor (to be just to him we judge, even him,

This Jew, whose presence makes the glad World dim)

That often to the martyr in his prison

He went and whisper'd ' Comfort ! I am risen ; '

Nor that to sickbeds sad, as Death came near,

He stole with radiant face and whisper'd cheer,

And to the Crucified brought secretly

The vinegar and sponge of Charity !

Yet in the name of those who died for Him,

Self-slain, or by the beasts rent limb from limb,

Who in his Name with calm unbated breath

Went smiling down the dark descent of Death,

Who went because He beckon'd with bright hand

Out of the mirage of a heavenly Land,

I demand justice on their Christ, this Jew !

Pass on.   From land to land the tidings flew

That Christ was God, and that the World was doom'd !

Then droopt the lilies of delight, then bloom'd

The martyr's rose of blood ; Kings on their thrones

Cast down their crowns and crawled with piteous moans

To the baptismal font where Priests, grown bold,

Held high the crucifix wrought round with gold.

And soon (how swiftly seeds of evil spring !)

They set a Priest on High and crowned him King,

Yea, King of all earth's Kings, and next to Christ !

There reign'd he, at his will the realms were priced,

And each, grown blind to worldly gain and loss,

Paid tribute to the King and to the Cross.

Behind that King, this Phantom most forlorn

Kept watch, from morn to night, from night to morn ;

And countless Temples rose into the air,

Golden and vast and marvellously fair,

And artists wrought on canvas and on stone

Strange images of Christ upon His Throne

Judging the World ; and voices filled each land :

' Rejoice—the heavenly Kingdom is at hand ; '

And for a space indeed, so well he feign'd,
It seem'd that Christ had conquer'd Death, and reigned.

The triumph passed.   The poison of the Lie ·
Spread, as all foul things spread beneath the sky ;
And presently, the time being ripe at last,
From shrine to shrine this pallid Phantom passed
Whispering, ' My Word hath grown a wingèd fire,
Yet thousands doubt me and blaspheme the Sire—
See ye to this, O Priests ! seek the abhorred
And judge them, with your Master's Flame and Sword.'

Look, where the culprit croucheth in his place,
Blood on his hands, and terror in his face !
Aye, glue your gaze upon him, while I tell
Of damnèd deeds and thoughts befitting Hell ! . . . .
They went abroad, his Priests, like wolves that scent
Lambs in the fields, and slew the innocent ;
The holy Shepherds who in places green
To Isis sang and Thammuz songs serene

They found and slaughter'd, till their red blood ran

In torrents down the streams Egyptian ;

The gentle Souls who loved their mother Earth,

And wept because she had given the Monster birth,

They cast in cruel fire, and sacrificed

To appease the blood-thirst of this Jew, their Christ !

From land to land, from sea to sea, they fled,

And where they went the plains were strewn with
    dead.

Then, when all men knelt down and cried in pain

' Hosannah to the Lord—for Christ doth reign,'

When no man doubted, since he dared not doubt

Because of fiends that ringed him roundabout,

When no man breath'd in his own dwelling-house,

They paused a little time and held carouse,

With full cups pledging Christ ; but mark the rest !

While they in triumph revelled east and west,

He past 'mong them, his chosen, and distilled

A fatal poison in the cups they filled,

And when thro' vein and thew the poison crept,

Like wolves upon each other's throats they leapt,

Rending each other in their Master's sight.

Next, in the name of Love and Love's delight,

And in the name of pagans blest and blind

Who loved the old gods best for they were kind,

Of virgins who despite the fire and sword

Shrank from this Scourge and called on God the Lord,

Of haggard men who dared not draw their breath

Because they deem'd this man, not Christ, but Death ;

Yea, in the name of his own Priests profaned

Because they did his bidding, and he reigned,

I demand justice on their Christ, this Jew.

Nay, listen yet. The dark corruption flew

Like loathsome pestilence from land to land ;

From every Altar, raised at his command,

Blood dript like dew ; grown mad with pride and scorn

His Priests cast off the masks that they had worn,

And 'neath the Cross, within the very shrines,

Held hideous revel with their concubines,

Flaunted before their silent Christ thorn-crowned

The emblems of Priapus, and around

Danced naked, with lewd songs and signs obscene;

Then the bald monk, upon the convent green,

Rolled with the harlot; then the King of Priests

In the very Shrine did lewdness worse than beast's,

While Incest and foul Lusts without a name

Crawl'd in His temples, and he felt no shame.

For when the people murmur'd, Priests and Kings

Made answer, 'Be at peace, ye underlings!

Since 'tis enough to deem that Christ is Lord,

To adore his symbols and to wield his sword,

And all our deeds, tho' black as blackest night,

Are vindicated in our Master's sight!'

Oh, God that madest Man, if God there be,

Didst make these things, didst hear this blasphemy?

No writing on the wall disturbed the feasts

Of pathic Popes and leprous, lechrous Priests?

This Man with falsehoods seventy times seven

Defamed Thy world, and Thou wast dumb in Heaven!

Now, in the name of vestals sacrificed

To feed the lust of those same priests of Christ,

Of acolyte children tangled in the mesh

Of infamous and nameless filths of flesh,

In the name of those whom King and Priest and
  Pope

Cast down to dust, beyond all peace and hope,

Yea, in their names who made this Man their guide,

And curst by men, by him were justified,

I demand justice on their Christ, this Jew!

Pass on.   With cruel pitiless hand he drew

A curtain o'er the azure Heavens above,

Hiding the happy Light, darkening the love

Which kept life clean and whole ; so that in time

The very smile of Life became a crime

Against his Godhead !--Brother turn'd from brother,

The father smote his child, the son his mother,

And every fire that made home warm and sweet

Was trampled into ashes 'neath his feet.

Then cried he, 'Life itself is shame and sin!

Break ye all human ties, and ye shall win

My Realm beyond the grave!' and as he cried,

Mortals cast ashes on their heads and died,

The virgin deem'd that Love's own kiss defiled,

The mother's milk was poison'd for the child,

The father, worse than beasts who love their young,

Cast to the wolves the little ones who clung

Crying around his neck; the Anchorite

Turn'd from the sunshine and the starry light

And hid his head in ordures of self-prayer;

The naked Saint loomed black against the air

Upon his tower of Famine; and for the sake

Of this Man's promise, and the Lie he spake,

Nature itself became a blight and ban!

Nay, more! thro' all the world corruption ran

As from a loathsome corpse—in every clime

Disease and Pestilence did shed their slime,

Till human Life, once clean and pure and free,

Shrank 'neath the serpent-scales of Leprosy!

Now in the name of Life defiled and scorn'd,

Of hearts that broke because this Phantom warn'd,

Of weary mothers desolately dying

For sons whose hearts were hardened to their crying,

Of wives made husbandless and left unblest,

Of little children starving for the breast,

Of homes made desolate from sea to sea

Because he said 'Leave all, and follow me,'

I demand justice on their Christ, this Jew!

He reign'd where Peace had reign'd!—and no man knew

The World wherein he dwelt, nor sought to guess

The holy laws of Light and Happiness;

Yea, from our sight the beauteous Heavens were veil'd

And the Earth under them, while yet Man trail'd

His self-wrought chain across the fruitless lands

And tore his own pure flesh with impious hands.

Then from the depths of sorrow pale men came,

Who climb'd the heights and lit thereon the flame

Which scatter'd darkness and illumed the skies,

And on the stars they fixed their starry eyes

And measured their progressions, crying aloud

'This Phantom of the Christ is but a cloud

Veiling the glory of the Infinite?'

What then?   His creatures found them in the night

And smote them down, and with a fouler fire

Made for their martyred bones a funeral pyre

That did proclaim his glory and their despair!

Even thus the Martyr, Man, once the glad heir

Of Earth and Heaven, made with eyes to see

And sense to comprehend his Destiny,

Was bound and render'd blind, until he fell

To Darkness dimly lit by lights of Hell,

And there, bereft and desolate of all

That made him free, he felt his dungeon wall

And wail'd on God; and lo, at this man's nod,

His Priests and Kings appear'd, instead of God,

Saying 'Bow down, thou Slave, and cease thy strife,

Confessing on thy knees that Death is Life,

And Darkness, Light!'—and to his mouth they thrust

Their cruel Cross, defiled with blood and dust ;

And when he had testified in all men's sight

That Death was Life and Darkness heavenly Light,

Forth to the fire the shuddering wretch was brought,

And slaughter'd to the Lie. themselves had taught.

Now, in their names, the Souls of priceless worth,

Who glorified the lights of Heaven and Earth,

Who fathom'd Nature's secret star-sown ways

And read the law of Life with fearless gaze,

Yet, for reward, with fire were shrivell'd up,

Or poison'd by the fatal hemlock-cup,

I demand doom and justice on this Jew !

Pass o'er the rest—the countless swarms he slew

To appease his lust for life in every land ;

The happy Nations stricken by his hand

With Famine or with Pestilence ;—the horde

Of butchering Tyrants and of Priests abhorred

Who fatten'd on the flesh and blood of men,

Because this Jew had died and risen again !

Come to the issue.   Hear it, Jew, and know

Nature hath gather'd strength to lay thee low !

Humanity itself shall testify

Thy Kingdom is a Dream, thy Word a Lie,

Thyself a living canker and a curse

Upon the Body of the Universe !

For lo, at last, thy Judge, the Spirit of Man,

And I, his Acolyte since Time began,

Have taught thy brethren, things of clay like thee,

That all thy promise was a mockery ;

That Fatherhood and Godhead there is none,

No Father in Heaven and in Earth no Son,

That Darkness never can be Light, that still

Death shall be Death, despite thy wish or will,

That Death alone can comfort souls bereaven

And shed on Earth the eternal sleep of Heaven.

Yet not until the weary world is free

Of all thy ghostly godhead, and of thee,

Shall he who stills all tumult and all pain

Unveil the happy Heavens once more, and reign ! '

He ceased, and Jesus heard, but made no sign.

Then, gazing sadly on that Man Divine,

He added, ' Peace, and hearken yet, O Jew !

For what we come to judge, we pity too !

The blessèd sleep Death sheds from sea to sea,

Shared by thy brethren, may be shared by thee,

If he who sits in Judgment deems it well ! '

While on those silent hosts his dark eyes fell,

And thro' the Waves of Life that darkly roll'd

Around him, ran a tremor deathly cold,

He cried, ' Awake, awake, for 'tis the time !

Appear, ye Witnesses of this Man's crime ! '

VIII

THE WITNESSES

First to the front a shrouded figure crept,
Gazed upon Jesus, hid his face, and wept,
Saying ' What would ye ?   Wherefore am I taken
Out of the dark grave where I slept forsaken,
Forgetting all my heritage of woe ? '

' What Soul art thou ? '

                         ' One Judas, named also
Iscariot.'

                    ' Know'st thou the Accused ? '

                                        ' Aye me,
In sooth I know him, to my misery !

I followed him, and I believed for long

That he was God indeed, serene and strong;

Then, with an eager hunger famishing

To see his Kingdom and to hail him King,

I did betray him, thinking " when he stands

Bound and condemn'd in the oppressor's hands,

When Death comes near to drink his holy breath,

He will put forth his power and vanquish Death ! "

But when I saw him conquer'd, crucified,

I hid my face in shame, then crept aside,

And in the Potter's Field myself I hung.'

' Now answer ! Was thy spirit conscience-stung ?

Having betrayed him, wherefore didst thou die ? '

' Because I knew his promise was a lie,

Because I knew the Man whom I had slain

Was *not* Messiah—Now, let me sleep again ! '

' Pass by. The next ! '

Forth stept before their sight
A form so old, so wan and hoary white,
It seem'd another Christ, as old, as sad;
And he in antique raiment too was clad,
Ragged and wild, and his white hair was strewn
Like snow around him 'neath the wintry Moon,
And by his side a lean she-bear there ran,
Gentle and tame, uplooking at the man
With piteous bleats, while his thin hand was spread
With touch as chill as ice upon its head.
When on the Accused this old Man turned his eyes
He shook and would have fled with feeble cries,
But a hand held him.   Shivering and afraid,
He shrank and gazed upon the ground, but stay'd.

'Thy name?'

'AHASUERUS.   Far away,
Beyond the changes of the night and day,
In the bleak regions of the Frozen Zone,

Lit with auroral beams, I roamed alone,

When a voice called me, and behold I came.'

' Look on the Accused.   Know'st thou his Form and
    Name ? '

' Alack, I know him, as I know my doom —

To wander o'er the world without a tomb,

Alone, unpitied, hopeless, weak and wild . . .

Before my door I stood with wife and child

That weary moment when they led him by,

Bearing his heavy Cross of Wood, to die.

He would have rested at my dwelling place,

But knowing him blasphemer, branded base,

Taking the name of God in vain, I cried,

" If thou art God, now cast thy Cross aside,

And take thy Throne—if thou hast lied, pass on ! "

He turned on me his face all woe-begone,

And murmur'd faintly, as he crawl'd away,

" *Thou* shalt not rest until my Judgment Day !

Till then walk on from sleepless year to year ! "

He spake. That doom pursued me. I am here.'

' Take comfort, brother. Tho' thy wrongs are deep,
When this same Jew is judgèd thou shalt sleep.
Pass by.'

         With feeble moan and weary pace
He went. Another stept into his place.

' Thou ? '

         ' PILATE, to whose Roman judgment seat
They brought this Jew, casting him at my feet
And clamouring for his life. I smiled to see
So mad a thing usurping sovereignty,
And said, " O Jews, if so ye list, fulfil
The law, and spare or slay him as ye will—
The Roman wars not with such foes as he—
Upon your heads, not mine, this deed shall be."
And ere to shameful Death the man was borne,
I turned aside and washed my hands in scorn
Of them and *him* ! '

' Pass on ! '

The Roman cast

One pitying look upon the Jew, and passed

Into the darkness.—As he sank from sight

There came in pale procession thro' the night

Great Phantoms who the imperial robe did wear,

Sceptre in hand, and bayleaves in the hair,

Each lewd and horrible and infamous,

A monster, yet a man : Tiberius,

Sejanus, and the rest ; and last of all

Came one who trode the earth with light foot-fall,

And sang with shrill voice to a golden lute ;

And lo ! a woman's robe from head to foot

Enwrapt him, and his face was sickly white

With nameless infamies of lewd delight,

And on his beardless cheeks mine eyes could see

The hideous crimson paint of harlotry,

While, in a voice as any eunuch's shrill,

He cried,

' This Jew, their Christ, lay cold and still

Within his Sepulchre, and slept supine,

While I, the Antichrist, pour'd blood like wine

To appease my parasites and paramours !

Nay, more, before my shining palace-doors

And round the gardens of the feast, I placed

The naked forms of men and maidens chaste

Who worshipt him, and lit the same to be

The living torches of my revelry;

And all in vain, thus stript and sacrificed,

They called on Christ to conquer Antichrist !

In the amphitheatre I sat and smiled

On strong men martyred and on maids defiled ;

Then clad myself in skins of beasts, and flew

To glut my lechery in all men's view,

And ravenous-claw'd my bestial lust I fed

On shuddering flesh of virgins ravishèd.

And yet he rose not ! Still and stark he lay.

God-like I reign'd, with a god's power to slay,

Shame, sadden, gladden. To the old Gods I sang

My triumph-song that thro' the nations rang

While Rome was burning! On my mother's womb
I thrust the impious heel! Yet from his tomb
This Jesus stirr'd not! God-like still, I died
By mine own hand, not shamed and crucified
As he, this Jew, had been!—He lives, ye say?
Poor Phantom of the Cross, forlorn and grey,
What shall his life avail? His day hath fled,
But other Antichrists uplift the head
And laugh, and cry " The reign of Christ is o'er!
Make merry! "—Yea, the Earth is his no more,
His Heaven a Dream, and where he wrought in vain
The harlot and the sodomite still reign!'

He spake, and with a shrill and cruel cry
Followed his brethren; in his track crept by
Pale ghostly Phantoms filleted or crown'd,
Imperial harlots with their zones unbound,
And haggard children clutch'd yet uncaress'd,
Rolling blind eyes and fighting for the breast;
And after these, a throng of martyrs slain,

Bloody and maim'd and worn, who wail'd in pain,

Fixing their piteous eyes on that pale Jew.

Crowd after crowd they passed, and passing threw

A curse or prayer on Him who anguish'd there

Crown'd with the calm of a divine despair,

And one by one he mark'd them come and go

While down his wrinkled cheeks deep-sunk in woe

The salt tears ran, and ever and anon

He hid his face so weary and woe-begone,

Or peering vaguely up into the Night

Pressèd his skinny hands together tight

And moan'd unto himself!

IX

THEN saw I rise

A shape with broad bold brow and fearless eyes,

Behind him as he came a murmuring train

Of augurs, soothsayers, and armèd men,

With gentle priests of Ceres and of Pan.

'Room there,' they cried aloud, 'for Julian!'

Bareheaded, helm in hand, he took his place

Before the Accused, a smile upon his face.

'Thy name was JULIAN?'

He answered, 'Yes!

I wore the imperial robe in gentleness,

And looking on the World around my throne

I heard the wretched weep, the weary moan,

Saw Nature sickening because this Man wrought

To scatter poison in the wells of Thought,

So that no Soul might live in peace and be

Baptised in wisdom and philosophy;

Wherefore I summoned from their lonely graves

The Spirits of the mountains and the waves,

The tutelary Sprites of flowers and trees,

The rough wild Gods and naked Goddesses,

And all alive with joy they leapt around

My leaf-hung chariot, to the trumpet's sound!

Yea, and I wakened from ancestral night

The human shapes of Healing and of Light—

Asclepios with his green magician's rod,

And Aristotle, Wisdom's grave-eyed god,

And bade them teach the natural law and prove

The eternal verities of Life and Love.

What then? I fail'd. This Serpent could elude

My priests, however swiftly they pursued,

And since I warned them not to slay with steel

Nor bruise it cruelly beneath the heel,

It lived amid their very footprints, fed

On blood and tears, upraised the impious head,

Then last, still living on my day of doom,

Stung my pale corpse and coil'd upon my tomb!

Oh, had I guessed that mercy could not win

Blood from the stone, or change the Serpent's skin,

That pity and loving kindness ne'er could gain

Foothold in Superstition's black domain,

Then surely I the avenging sword had bared

And slain in mercy what I blindly spared!

'Twas but a spark! one stamp of foot, and lo!

The thing had perished!   Fool, to let it grow!

So that it grew as such foul hell-fire can,

Spreading from City unto City of Man,

Turning this World of greenness and sweet breath

Into a charnel house of shameful Death.

The Galilean conquered as I threw

My last wild jet of life-blood to the blue,

Nature resigned her birth-right with a groan,

And Thought, like Niobe, was turn'd to stone!'

G

His legions shouted faintly as he cast

One glance of scorn on the pale Jew and passed

To darkness.   Following him, methought, there stalked

Aurelius, calmly musing as he walked,

With many another lesser King of clay,

Who paused and testified, then passed away ;

So thick they came from out the troubled dark

My brain grew dizzy and I ceased to mark,

Until at last a marble Maiden rose,

Stript naked to the skin and bruised with blows,

Yet fair and golden-haired and azure-eyed

She stood erect with fearless gaze, and cried :

' I was HYPATIA.   Round my form fell free

The white robe of a wise virginity,

While in the fountains of the Past I sought

Strange pearls of Dream and dim Platonic thought.

Now, as I gazed therein, I saw full plain

The faces of dead Gods whom men had slain—

How fair they seemed ! how gentle and how wise !

The Spirits of the gladsome earth and skies !

And lo, I loved them, and I lit anew

Their vestal lamps that men might love them too,

And so be passionately purified.

The rest ye know.   Thro' this same Jew, I died.

Peter the Reader and his monkish throng

Found me and slew me, trail'd my limbs along

The streets, and left me, bloody, stark, and dead ! '

I watch'd her as with slow and silent tread,

Erect tho' naked, cloth'd with chaste cold Light

As is the virgin votaress of the Night,

She vanished in the darkness.   Then for long

I marked the Witnesses in shadowy throng

Come, say their say, and go ; from every side

They gathered one by one and testified,

And as they testified against the Jew

Creation darkened and the murmur grew !

Meantime the Accused stood listening, with his eyes

Fixed ever sadly on the far-off skies

Where flocks of patient stars moved slowly, driven
By winds unseen to the dark folds of Heaven,—
And ever as his gaze upon it yearned
The blue Void quicken'd and new splendours burned,
And while the lights of all the stars were shed
As lustrous dew upon his hoary head,
He knelt and prayed !

                   Then rose a mighty cry
Which shook the solid air and rent the sky,
And flowing thither came a countless crowd
Of women and of men who called aloud
' Allah il Allah ! '—Darkening under Heaven,
Like to the waves of Ocean tempest-driven,
Out of the midnight I beheld them come
Up to the Judgment Seat and break to foam
Of dusky faces and of waving hands ;
And many raised aloft great crookèd brands
And banners where the moonlike crescent burn'd.
Then dimly thro' the darkness I discern'd

A stately turban'd King, who stood alone ;

Around his form a prophet's robe was thrown,

And in his hand he bore a scimitar

Unsheath'd and shining radiant like a star ;

And on his head there shone a crescent gem,

Bright as the moon ; and to his raiment hem

Clung women, naked, glorious-eyed, and fair,

Houris of Heaven with perfumed golden hair.

And the great Sea of Life, that raged and broke

Behind him, sank to silence as he spoke,

Awed by the gleam of his dark eyes ; for lo !

He paused not, but moved onward proud and slow,

Saying, as past the Judgment Seat he strode,

' This man cried, " I am Allah ! very God ! "

Yet helpless as a slaughter'd lamb he fell

Beneath the angry breath of Azraèl,

Great Allah's Angel, sent to avenge his Lord !

But I, who raised alike the Cross and Sword,

In Allah's name, his Prophet, was content

To avow myself the man by Allah sent

To do his will in proud humility.

So men forgot this Jew, and turn'd to me,

Who on the desert-sands my flag unfurled

And wrought great miracles to amaze the world !

Upon the neck of Kings my foot was set,

And all the Nations knew me—Mahomet ! '

And at the name the echoing millions roar'd

' Allah il Allah !—Mighty is the Lord !

Mahomet is his prophet ! '   Cloud on cloud,

Wave following wave, with clash of tumult loud,

The mighty Sea of Lives passed onward, crying,

' Allah il Allah ! ' and ever multiplying ;

And when the far-off western horizon

Was darkened yet with those who had come and gone,

Millions still came from the eastward, sweeping by

The Judgment Seat with that victorious cry ;—

And endless seem'd the space of time until

The swarms had past, and all again was still,—

When, fronting the Accused, the Accuser cried :

'Greater than this pale Jew men crucified

Was he whose mighty star, blood-red and bright,

Shines on the minarets of the Islamite ! '

But as he spake, out of the East there came

One follow'd, too, with clangorous acclaim—

A human Shape, wrapt in white lamb-like wool,

Star-eyed and sad and very beautiful,—

A sceptre in his hand, and on his head

A crown of silver, brightly diamonded ;

Who, flying swift as wind on veilèd feet,

Approach'd, and pausing at the Judgment Seat,

Cried :

      ' Sleeping in my Sepulchre, wherein

I deem'd myself secure from sense and sin,

A voice disturbed me, and awakening,

I heard wild voices o'er the Nations ring,

Naming the names of lesser gods than I.

Deathless I pause, while all the rest pass by—

They taught them how to live, I taught them how to die !

Heir of the realms of sorrow and despair,

I, GAUTAMA, the BUDDHA, gently bare

The Lily, and not the Cross, and not the Sword,

And countless hailed me King and Lord!

What voices break my rest? What impious strife

Stirreth my sleep and brings me back to life?—

Yea, plucks me from God's breast, whereon I lay,

To take my place again 'mong Kings of clay,

Inheritors of Sorrow!'

                                        Even as
He spake, the throngs who follow'd bent like grass
Wind-blown to worship him!

                                        With radiant head
He passed on, follow'd by the Quick and Dead.

And in that train I saw, or seem'd to see,

Other inheritors of Deity—

His Brethren, Gods or God-like, following:

Pale ZOROASTER, crownèd like a King;

Menù and Moses, each with radiant look

Cast on the pages of an open Book ;

Confucius, in a robe of saffron hue,

Enwrought with letters quaint of mystic blue ;

Prometheus, dragging yet his broken chain,

And gazing heavenward still, in beautiful disdain.

Ghostwise they testified and vanishèd,

These mighty spirits of the god-like Dead ;

Some reverend and hoary, some most fair,

With brightness in their eyes and on their hair,

Each kingly in his place, and in his train

Souls of fair worshippers that Jew had slain.

X

Then, waiting on and watching thro' the gloom,

I saw the glimmer of an open Tomb

Hewn in the mountain-side, and thence a band

Crown'd and tiara'd, each with Cross in hand,

Of woeful Phantoms issued, murmuring :

' We were the Vicars of this Christ, our King !

And lo, he let us reign !—and sins like lice

Ran o'er us, while we sought with foul device

To cloak the living Lie on which we fed ! '

And one cried : ' As I lay upon my bed,

My leman at my side, mine hands still red

With mine own brother's blood, they strangled me ! '

And one laugh'd, ' With this Cross as with a key

I open'd up the caves where Monarchs kept
Their secret gold ! '

              And one who wail'd and wept,
Yet could not speak, gaped with black jaws forlorn
To show the mouth whence the red tongue was torn.

And one said, ' Murder was my handmaiden !
I made a Throne with bones of butcher'd men
And set her there, and in my Master's name
Baptised her ! ' And all those others cried again—
' We were his Vicars, and he bade us reign ! '

Back to the Tomb they crept with senile cries,
Mumbling with toothless gums and blinking eyes
Thick with the rheum of age !—and in their stead
Rose shapes of butcher'd Seers whose wounds still bled,
And some were clothen with consuming flame
As with a garment, crying as they came :
' We saw all Nature blacken'd far and wide
Because this Jew was dead yet had not died,

For thro' the world of broken hearts he went

Demanding blood and tears for sacrament,

Crowning the proud and casting down the just,

Lighting the altar-flames of Pride and Lust,

Calling the Deadly Sins accurst and dire

To be his acolytes and to feed the fire

Through which we perish'd ; yet we testified

With all our Souls against him ere we died ! '

O Night of terror ! O dark suffering Night,

With wounded bleeding heart and great eyes bright

With starry portents and serene despairs !

I saw them, one by one, the ghostly heirs

Of Wisdom and of Woe, the Souls long fled

Who died like him, and like him are not dead,

The Great, the Just, the Good, who cannot die,

Because this piteous Phantom passeth by,

And when they fain would slumber, murmureth

' Lo, Christ is God, and God hath vanquish'd Death ! '

Like wave on wave they came, like cloud on cloud.

Before the Throne stood one wrapt in his shroud,

And bearing in his lean uplifted hand,

That shook but did not fall, a flaming Brand.

The Judge spake (while I dream'd who this might be)

' Thy name ? '

       ' GALILEO, of Italy,'

He answer'd ; while two other shapes in white

Crept to him, on the left hand and the right.

' These Brethren, standing side by side with me,

Wore the white raiment of Philosophy,

Yet died in anguish, butcher'd in Christ's name.

He on my right hand, BRUNO, died by flame.

He on my left, CASTILIO, starved for bread.

We saw the Heavenly Book above us spread,

We pored upon its living lines of fire,

And saw therein the Name of God the Sire.

Upon us as we ponder'd, thought, and prayed,

Came this man's Priests and Soldiers, and betrayed

Our Souls to torture and to infamy ! '

' 'Tis well.   Ye kept your Souls sublime and free,

And he who slew you waits for judgment *there* ! '

Suddenly, with a shriek that rent the air,

Shadows on shadows throng'd around and cried :

' *We*, too, were slain because we testified !

Our bones are scattered white in every land !

We pass'd the Fiery Torch from hand to hand ;

Fast as one fell, another raised it high,

Till he in turn was smitten down to die.

Yet on, from clime to clime, from pole to pole,

It pass'd, and lit the Beacons of the Soul,

Till wheresoever men could gaze they saw

The fiery signs and symbols of the Law,

Older than God, which saith the Soul is free ! '

The Accuser smiled, and rising quietly,

With ominous lifted hand, ' O Judge,' he cried,

' If I should question all men who have died

Because this Jew once quickened in the sun,

Eternity would pass ere all was done.

Enough to know, wherever men have striven

To read the open scrolls of Earth and Heaven,

Wherever in their sadness they have sought

To find the stainless flowers of lonely Thought,

Raising the herb of Healing and the bloom

Of Love and Joy, this Man from out his Tomb

Hath stalk'd, and slaying the things their souls deem'd
fair

Hath poison'd all their peace and stript them bare.

Century on century, as men count Time,

This Man hath been a curse in every clime ;

So that the World, once the glad home of men,

Hath been a prison and a lazar-den,

A place of darkness whence no Soul might dare

To seek the golden Earth and heavenly air,

Save fearfully, with panting lips apart,

Fearing the very throb of his own heart

As 'twere a death-knell ; nay, this Jew set free

Disease and Pestilence and Leprosy

To crawl like loathsome monsters and destroy

Great Cities once alive with life and joy ;

And of all foul things fouler than the beasts

Were this Man's Servants and approven Priests,

Stenching the Cities wheresoe'er they trod,

Poisoning the fountains in the name of God.

Save for this Jew, a thousand years ago

Man might have known what he awakes to know—

The luminous House of flesh and blood most fair,

Rainbow'd from dust and water and sweet air,

The green Earth round it, and the Seas that roll

To cleanse the Earth from shining pole to pole,

The Heavens, and Heavens beyond without a bound,

The Stars in their processions glory-crown'd,

Each star so vast that it transcends our dreams,

So small, a child might grasp it, so it seems,

Like a light butterfly ! The wondrous screed

Of Nature open lay for Man to read ;

World flashed to world, in yonder Void sublime,

The messages of Light and Change and Time ;

The Sea had voices, and the Spirit of Earth

Had sung her mystic runes of Death and Birth,

Of all the dim progressions Life had known,

And writ them on the rocks in words of stone;

Nay, Man's own Soul was as a mirror, bright

With luminous changes of the Infinite!

And yet Man rested blind beneath the sky

Because this Jew said, ' Close thine eyes, or die!'

Enough—pass onward one by one, ye throng

Who sinn'd thro' Christ, or suffer'd shame and wrong;

Stay not to speak—your faces shall proclaim,

More loud than tongues, your martyrdom and shame!'

Ghostwise they passed along before my sight,

Martyrs of truth and warriors of the right,

Some reverend and hoary, some most fair

With sunrise in their eyes and on their hair.

So swift they came and fled, I scarce had space

To note them, but full many a world-famed face

Came like a breaking wave and went again:

JUSTINIAN, living, yet a corpse, as when

They tore him from his tomb; old, gaunt, and grey,

The Master of the Templars, DU MOLAY,

Clasp'd by the harlot, Fire,—follow'd by pale

And martyr'd warriors bleeding 'neath their mail;

ABELARD, still erect on stubborn knees

Facing the storms of Rome, and ELOISE

Clad like an abbess, from his eyes of fire

Drinking eternal passion and desire;

KING FREDERICK, his step serene and strong

As if he trod on altars, with his throng

Of warriors, Christian and Saracen;

Great ALGAZALLI and wise ALHAZEN,

White-robed and calm, with many a lesser man

Wrapt in the peace of lore Arabian;

Pale PETRARCH, laurel-crownèd, gazing on

The white face of that sister woe-begone

Who thro' the lust of Christ's own Vicar fell;

JOHN HUSS, still wrapt around with fires of Hell,

Clutching the Book he bore with piteous tears.

Silent they pass'd, the Martyrs and the Seers,

Known and unknown, the Heirs of love and praise ;

And last, the Three, who with undaunted gaze

Faced the great Ocean of Earth's mystery,

Mighty and strong as when from sea to sea

They sail'd and sail'd ; DE GAMA, following

COLUMBUS, who with sea-bird's sleepless wing

Flew on from Deep to Deep ; and, mightiest,

MAGELLAN, faring forward on his quest,

Putting the craven cowls of Rome to shame,

And lighting Earth and Heaven with his resplendent

    name !

XI

With woe unutterable, and pity cast

As the still Heaven on which his eyes were cast,

That old Jew listen'd, while new voices cried,

' We too were slain, because we testified ! '

But as they pass'd along with waving brands

Beneath him, he outstretched his trembling hands

As if to bless them, murmuring low yet clear,

' Father in Heaven, where art Thou?   Dost Thou hear?

And at the voice those Spirits cried again,

' We testified against thee, and were slain ! '

And never down on them his eyes were turn'd,

But still upon the silent Heaven, that yearn'd

Its heart of stars out on his hoary head !

Even as a shipwrecked wight doth cling in dread

To some frail spar, and seèth all around

The dark wild waters swelling without bound,

While momently the black waves flash to foam,

Ev'n so I saw the Spirits go and come

With piteous cries around me.   From all lands

They gather'd, moaning low and waving hands,

Women and men and naked little ones ;

And some were dusky-hued from flaming suns

That light the West and East ; for lo, I knew

The hosts of Ind, the children of Peru,

And the black seed of Ham ; and following these,

Wan creatures bearing hideous images

Of wood and stone ; yellow and black and red,

They gather'd, murmuring as they came, and fled !

And all the air was troubled, as when the rain

Maketh the multitudinous leaves complain

In some deep forest solitude, with the stirs

Of tutelary gods and worshippers,

Of creatures thronging thick as ants to upbuild

Strange Temples, frail as ant-heaps, faintly filled

With the first gleams of godhead chill and grey,
Then crumbling into dust, and vanishing away !

Borne on a purple litter came a King
Gold-crown'd, with eager armies following
Swift-footed like the pard, crested with plumes
Of many-coloured birds, and deck'd with blooms
Of many-colour'd flowers ; and as he came
Choirs of dark maidens sang in glad acclaim,
' All hail to MONTEZUMA, King and Lord ! '
And round him dusky Priests kept fierce accord
Of drums and cymbals, till their lord was borne
Close to the Throne ; and on that Man forlorn
Fixing his sad, brown, antelope's eyes, and lying
Like to a stricken deer sore-spent and dying,
He cried :

       ' In the grassy West I reigned supreme
O'er a great Kingdom wondrous as a dream.
As high as Heaven rose my palaces,

And fair as Heaven was the light in these,

And out of gold I ate, and gold and gems

Cover'd me to the very raiment hems,

And gems and gold miraculously bright

Illumed my roofs and floors with starry light.

The wondrous lama-wool as white as milk,

More soft and snowy than the worm's thin silk,

Was woven for my raiment; unto me

The creatures of the Mountains and the Sea

Were brought in tribute; and from shore to shore

My naked couriers flew for ever, and bore

My mandate to the lesser Kings, my slaves;

Yea, and my throne was on a thousand graves,

And Death, obedient to my lifted hand,

Smiled peacefully upon a golden Land.

There, as I reigned, and millions blest my sway,

Came rumours of a fair God far away

Greater than those I worshipt, till my throne

Shook at the coming of that form unknown;

And o'er the Ocean, borne on flying things

That caught the winds and held them in their wings,

Riding on manèd monsters that obeyed

Bridles of gold and champ'd the bit and neigh'd,

Came this Man's followers, clad and shod with steel,

Trampling my naked hosts with armèd heel

And raising up the Cross ; and me they found

Within my shining palace sitting crown'd,

'Mid priests and slaves that trembled at my nod,

And bade me worship him, their pale white God,

Nailèd upon a Tree and crucified ;

And when upon mine own strong gods I cried,

They answer'd not ! nay, even when I was cast

Unto the dust, bound like a slave at last,

Still they were dumb; and tho' my people arose

Innumerable, they were scattered even as snows

Before the wintry blast ; with sword and spear

The bloody Spaniard hunted them like deer,

So that my realm ran blood in this Man's name ;

And lo ! my proud heart broken with its shame,

I died to all my glory, and lay mute,

Defiled, and scorn'd, beneath the Spaniard's foot,
And all my Kingdom fell to nothingness.'

He pass'd, and after him came Monarchs less
Than he, yet proud and mighty,—I watch'd them fly
Like flocks of antelopes beneath the sky,
And harrying them the Hunters clad in mail
Follow'd, with cruel faces marble pale,
Lifting the Cross, and speeding fast beyond
My sight, on steeds with gold caparison'd.

Nor ceased the pageant yet.   Sceptred and crown'd,
A King, with plumèd legions wailing round,
Stood up and cried :

         ' The splendour of the Sun
Illumed the Temples where my rites were done,
And to the Sun-god who for ever gazed
With face of gold upon my realm, I raised
The pæan and the prayer.   Beneath my rule

The happy lands grew bright and beautiful,

And countless thousands innocent of strife

Blest me, and that refulgent Fount of Life.

Fairer my palaces and temples far

In sight of Heaven than Morn or Even Star,

For in them dwelt the quickening Light of him

Before whose glory every sphere is dim !

Yea, but at last mine eyes did gaze upon

A blood-star, rising o'er the horizon

Out eastward, and before its baleful ray

The Sun-god shrivel'd and was driven away ;

And leagued with iron monsters belching fire,

And riding living monsters tame yet dire,

Out from the gulfs of sudden blackness pour'd

A mailèd band who called this man their Lord,

And slew us ev'n as sheep, and undertrod

The shining temples of the Sun, our God ;

Me too they smote and slaughter'd, offering me,

Last of the Incas, to their Deity—

And Darkness reign'd where once the Light had shone ! '

Wailing, he wrung his hands and wander'd on,

And after him like bleeding sheep a train

Of naked slaughter'd things that sob'd in pain—

Midst them a dusky woman richly drest,

Who wrung her hands and smote her naked breast,

Crying, ' I loved the soldier of this Jew,

And me he lusted for, then foully slew,

And wheresoe'er his Cross waved overhead

Came shrieks of women torn and ravishèd ! '

And round her as she spake those butcher'd bands

Of women smote their breasts or wrung their hands.

' O shadowy crowds of men,' the Accuser cried,

' Dark naked women, children piteous-eyed,

All manacled and bleeding, worn and weak,

How do ye testify against him ?   Speak ! '

' Because,' they said, ' the radiant summer Light

Had burnt our bodies and made them black yet bright,

Altho' our hearts within were sweet and mild,

We suffered sorrow, man and wife and child :

Far in the West we prayed, bending the knee

In Cities fairer far than Nineveh,

And high as Heaven arose fair palaces

Lit with the many colour'd images

Of gentle gods,—but on our shores there came

Devils that smote us in this white God's name,

Our gods dethroned, our temples overcast,

And scattered us as chaff before the blast.

This Jew looked on.   His Priests piled gold, while we

Were basely slain or sold to slavery ;

Tears worse than blood we shed, and bloodiest sweat,

While on the soil, with blood of millions wet,

They did upraise his Church, that rose on high

With fiery finger pointing at the sky

Where every happy star had ceased to shine ! '

XII

' Thou hearest, Jew ? '

But Jesus made no sign.

With woe unutterable and pity vast
As the still Heaven on which his eyes were cast,
He listen'd dumbly, while new voices cried,
' We too were slain, and by his Priests we died ! '
And like to cloud on cloud, blown by the wind
And broken, dusky swarms of Humankind
Still came and went ; and then rose wailing crowds
Who bare the lighted candle, and in their shrouds
Walk'd naked-footed to the martyr's pyre ;
With men whose entrails Famine's hidden fire
Gnaw'd till they shriek'd aloud ; and everywhere

A cruel scent of carnage filled the air,

As countless armèd legions of the slain

Roll'd up as if for battle once again,

While o'er them, flaming between earth and sky,

The crimson Cross was swung !

All these pass'd by ;

Then Silence deep as Death fell suddenly,

And all was hushèd as a rainy Sea !

Then came a rush of hosts mingled in storm

Confusedly, and phantoms multiform

That shriek'd and smote each other !

'Behold them,' cried

The Accuser, 'Followers of the Crucified !

The ravening wolves of wrath that never sleep,

Yet seek his fold and call themselves his sheep !

Where'er they strive, Murder and Madness dwell,

And Earth is lighted with the hates of Hell !

Lo, how they love each other, having heard
The crafty gospel of his broken Word!
Lo, how they surge in everlasting strife,
Seeking the mirage of Eternal Life!'

Struggling unto the Judgment place they came,
Smiting each other in their Master's Name;
Beneath their feet fell women stab'd and cleft,
And little children anguishing bereft.
And like a River of Blood that ever grew,
They rush'd until they roll'd round that pale Jew,
And lo! his feet grew bloody ere he was 'ware!
Yet still they smote each other, and in despair
Shriek'd out his praises as they multiplied
Their dead around him . . . And thus *they* testified!

And he, the Man Forlorn, stood mute in woe.

I saw the white corpse of the Huguenot
Float past him on that dreadful Sea of Lives;

I saw the nun struck down and gash'd with knives
Ev'n as she told her beads; I saw them pass,
The Martyrs of the Book or of the Mass,
Cast down and slain alike; the priest of Rome
Fought with the priest of Luther, thrusting home
With venomous knife or sword; and evermore
The Cross of Blood was wildly waven o'er
The waves of carnage, till they swept from sight,
Moaning and rushing onward thro' the Night.

Then, as the Storm seem'd weeping itself away,
I saw two ghostly Spirits looming grey
Against that dark Golgotha, and one of these
Clung to the other, and sank upon his knees.

'What man art *thou*?'

      'JEAN CALAS.'

          'He whose hands
Thou, kneeling, wettest with thy tears; who stands
Smiling upon the Accused?'

The last replied :

'VOLTAIRE the people named me. I denied

The godhead of that Jew, and at his brow

Pointed in mockery and scorn, as now !

Pope, Kings, and Priests shiver'd like frighten'd birds

Before the rain and lightning of my words,

And crouch'd with draggled plumage, awed and dumb,

Because they deem'd that Antichrist had come.

One day I heard this man in his poor home

Shriek loud, encircled by the snakes of Rome ;

And tho' their poison slew him, ere he died

I crush'd the vipers 'neath my heel, and cried

" Thy woes shall be avengèd ; *I* am here ! "

Even then a million wretches cast off fear,

And looking on this man's seed, redeem'd by me,

Fear'd the foul Christ no longer, and grew free ! '

Thin, gaunt and pale, around his lips the ray

Of a cold scorn, he smiled and passed away,

His eyes upon the Jew ; and with him went

I

Dark silent men whose musing eyes were bent

On open scrolls; and 'mong them laughing stood

A King who held a mimic Cross of wood,

And broke it o'er his knee, with a fierce jest;

So pass'd they, Holbach, Diderot, and the rest,

The foes of Godhead and the friends of Man;

But after them great crowds in tumult ran,

Who waved their dark and blood-stain'd arms and
    shrieked,

' We, who had lain in darkness, rose and wreak'd

Man's wrath on this false God, who had scorn'd our
    prayer

And sent his Kings and Slaves to strip us bare!

Yea, in his Name the Harlots and the Priests

Yoked us and harness'd us like blinded beasts;

And when we cried for food they profferèd

The stones of his cold Gospel and not bread;

And where his blessing fell the foul found gold,

And where it fell not we were bought and sold.

His foot was on the heads beneath him bowed,

His hand was with the pitiless and the proud,

His mercy failed us, but the curse he gave

Pursued our spirits even beyond the grave.

Thus he who had promised love gave only hate !

He spake of Heaven and made Earth desolate !

Thou didst at last avenge us, Spirit of Man,

Through thee the Night was cloven and Day began,

And on thine altars blood as sacrament

Appal'd the Kings of Earth this God had sent ! '

Then once again the Accuser rose and cried :

' The countless hosts of Dead have testified ;

But lastly, to this solemn Judgment-place,

I summon up the seed of this Man's race ;

Bear witness now, ye Jews, against this Jew !

XIII

THEN instantly, as if some swift hand drew

A curtain back, the darkness of the Night

Was cloven, and thronging in the starry light

New legions of the ghostly Dead appear'd,

And ever, as the Judgment Seat they near'd,

They shriek'd ' MESSIAH ! ' and with lips apart,

Startled as if a knife had prick'd his heart,

That pale Jew listen'd, and his wan face turn'd

To those who cried ; but when those hosts discern'd

His human lineaments, they shriek'd anew

' One God we worship, and this Man we slew,

Seeing he took the Holy Name in vain !

And since that hour that he was justly slain,

His hate hath follow'd us from place to place !

Wherefore, O Judge, we, children of his race,

Scorn'd, tortured, shamed, defamed, defiled, and driven
Outcast from every gate of Earth or Heaven,
Still martyr'd living and still dishonour'd dead,
Demand thy wrath and judgment on his head,
Jesus the Jew, not Christ, but Antichrist!'

Dumb as a lamb brought to be sacrificed,
Helpless and bound, He listen'd—still with gaze
Fix'd on the starry azure's pathless ways,
But down his cheeks, furrow'd with weary years,
Slowly and softly fell the piteous tears.

Like hordes of wolves, fierce, foul, and famishing,
That round some lonely Traveller shriek and spring,
Black'ning the snows around his lonely path,
Rending each other in their hungry wrath,
The children of the Ghetto, gathering there,
His brethren, fed their eyes on his despair
And spat their hate upon him ; and the snow
Was sooted with these nameless shapes of woe ;

But hither and thither, 'mid the ravening horde,

Moved Rabbis who lookt upward and adored

The Lord of Hosts, with hoary Saints and Seers,

And dark-eyed Maids who sang with sobs and tears

Of God's bright City overthrown in shame,

Jerusalem the Golden !—and at the Name

The woeful throngs who roll'd in tumult by

Rent robes, and wail'd, and echoed back the cry

' Jerusalem ! Jerusalem ! '—and lo !

From 'midst the multitudinous ebb and flow

That ever came and went, there did arise

A Prophet, with white beard and burning eyes,

Saying, ' Holy, Holy still, thy Name shall be,

Jerusalem, thro' God's Eternity !

For tho' thy glory hath fallen, and thy gate

Lies broken, and thy streets are desolate,

And on thy head ashes and dust are flung,

And in thy folds the wolf suckles her young,

Thou shalt arise in splendour and in pride,

And we, thy people, shall be justified !

Our tents are scattered, and our robes are riven,

Like chaff before the blast our race hath driven

In darkness, ever homeless, thro' the lands,

But never another City by our hands

Hath been upbuilded, since where'er we roam

Thou, City of God, art still our Hope and Home!

And tho' with bitterest tears our eyes are dim,

We hearken ever for the call of Him

Who thunder'd upon Sinai! . . . In thy breast

This Snake who stings thee still doth make his nest!

This Son who smote thee, Mother, still doth lie

Within thine arms ; but o'er thee, yonder on high,

Watches the God of Jacob!   Patience yet!

Tho' for a little space thy sun hath set,

As red as blood it shall arise again

For vengeance, and the God of Wrath shall reign,

With thee, his Bride long chosen, and over us,

Thy children ! '

                Thronging multitudinous,

With one great voice they answered : ' Holy be

Thy Name, Jerusalem, thro' Eternity ! '

And now their wailings sobb'd themselves to calm,

While to a sound of harps and lutes the psalm

Of Israël rose to Heaven—' *Holy be*

Thy Name, Jerusalem, thro' Eternity ! '

XIV

THEN said that Form who sat in Judgment :

'Jew !

Once judged and slain, yet risen and judged anew,

Thou hast heard the Accuser and his Witnesses.

Hast thou a word to utter answering these ?

Hast thou a living Soul beneath the sky

To rise upon thy side and testify ?

Summon thy Witnesses, if such there be,

Ere I pronounce the doom of Man on thee ! '

The Jew gazed round, and wheresoe'er his gaze

Shed on that throng its gentle suffering rays,

Tumult and wrath were hush'd, as in deep Night

Great waves lie down to lap the starry light

And lick the Moon's cold feet that touch the Sea.

'I have no word to answer,' murmured He,

' The winter of mine age hath come, and lo !

My heart within sinks 'neath its weight of woe !

So faint and far-removed all seems to be,

I seem the ghost of mine own Deity,

The apparition of myself, and not

A living thing with will or strength or thought !

Yet I remember (here his piteous eyes

Search'd the bare Heavens again with dim surmise),

Yet I remember, on this my Judgment Day,

Not what is near, but what is far away.

Within my Father's House I fell to sleep

In dreamless slumber mystical and deep,

And when I waken'd, to mine own faint crying,

Above the cradle small where I was lying

A Mother's face hung like a star, and smiled.

' Transform'd into the likeness of a child,

Feebly I drank the milk of mortal being ;

But as the green world brightened to my seeing

And the round arc of air closed over me,

The Land beyond grew dark to memory,

And I forgot my former dwelling-place,

The Life Eternal, and my Father's Face.

Closer and darker, as the summers flew,

The folds of flesh around my spirit grew,

Shutting that heavenly Mansion from my sight,

Save oftentimes in visions of the night

When for a space I slept the sleep of earth ;

But since that moment of my mortal birth,

I have not seen my Father, and now he seems

More faint than any form beheld in dreams ! '

He paused, uplifting still his weary gaze

To search the empty Heaven's pathless ways

For miracle and token, then was dumb.

' Thy quest hath fail'd, thy Kingdom hath not come,

The dark Judge said ; ' thy promise was a Lie—

Thy Witnesses ? '

And Jesus made reply :
‘ Hosts of the happy Dead whom I have blest ! ’

‘ Call—let them come ! ’

‘ I would not break their rest.’

‘ Thou hast lied to them, O Jew ! ’ the dark Judge cried.

And Jesus said, ‘ O Judge, I have not lied ! ’

‘ False was thy promise—false and mad and drear.
There is no Father ! ’

‘ Father, dost Thou hear ? ’

‘ Enough—renew thy miracles, and prove
Thy words, O Jew !   From yonder Void above
Summon the Form, the Face, in all men’s eyes,
And we absolve thee ! ’

On the starry skies,

Still thinly shrouded with the falling snow,

He fix'd his wistful gaze, and answer'd low,

' I bide my Father's time ! '

XV

THEN, as he bent
His brow like one who kneels for sacrament,
And on his feeble form and hoary head
The benediction of the Night was shed,
Methought I saw a Shape behind him stand,
Grim as a godhead graven in brass, his hand
Uplifted, and his wrinkled face set stern,
While terrible his deep black eyes did burn
In scornful wrath.   Naked as any stone
He stood, save for a beast's skin loosely thrown
Around his dusky shoulders, and he said :

' Thy Witnesses ?—Lord of the Quick and Dead,
Call them, and they shall come !   *I* first, who stood
And prophesied by Jordan's rolling flood,

And saw thee shining o'er the throng on me,

Thro' the white cloud of thy Humanity,

And knew thee in a moment by those eyes

Full of the peace of our lost Paradise !

Master and Lord of Life, these hands of mine

Baptized thee, blest thee, hailed thee most Divine,

Long promised, the Messiah !—and tho' thy brow

Is furrowed deep with years, I know thee now,

And in the name of all thou wast and art,

God's substance, of the living God a part,

Bear witness still, as I bare witness then,

Before this miserable race of men ! '

Then saw I, as he ceased and stood aside,

Another Spirit fair and radiant-eyed,

Who, creeping thither, at the Jew's feet fell,

And looking up with love ineffable

Cried ' Master ! ' and I knew that I beheld,

Tho' his face, too, was worn and grey with eld,

That other John whom Jesus to his breast

Drew tenderly, because he loved him best !

But even as I gazed, my soul was stirred

By other Shapes that stole without a word

Out of the silent dark, and kneeling low

Stretchèd out loving hands and wept in woe:

The gentle Mother of God grown grey and old,

Her silver hair still thinly sown with gold,

Mary the wife, and Mary Magdalen

Who murmur'd 'Lord, behold thy Handmaiden,'

And kiss'd his feet, her face so sadly fair

Hid in the shadows of her snow-strewn hair ;

And close to them, as thick as stars, appear'd

Faces of children brightening as they near'd

The presence of their Father ; and following these

Pallid Apostles falling upon their knees,

Crying ' Messiah !—Master—we are here ! '

As some poor famish'd wight doth take good cheer

Seeing an open door and one who stands

Upon the threshold with outstretchèd hands

That welcome him to some well-laden board,

That Wanderer brightened, while they murmur'd

    ' Lord !

We are thy Witnesses in all men's sight ! '

Feebly yet happily he rose his height,

And even as a Shepherd grave and old

Who smiles upon his flock within the fold,

He shone upon them till that sad place seemed

Fair as a starry night ; and still they stream'd

Out of the shadows, passionately crying

Upon the Name Beloved and testifying,

Till the dark Earth forgot its sorrowing

And grew as glad as Heaven opening !

Then one cried (and I knew him, for his face

Was dark and proud, yet lit with dews of grace,

And like an organ's peal his strong voice rang

With solemn echoes as of Saints that sang),

' Thy Witnesses ?   Father of all that be,

K

I persecuted those who followed thee,

Thy remnant, till thy fire from out the sky

Smote me, and as I fell I heard thee cry,

" Saul, Saul ! "—and shook as at the touch of Death ;

But on my face and eyelids came thy breath

To make me whole; and lo ! I sheathed the sword,

And girded up my loins to preach thy Word.

And the World listen'd, while the heathen praised

Thy glory, and believed ; and I upraised

Temples of marble where thy flocks might pray,

And where no Temple was from day to day

I made the Earth thy Temple, and the sky

A roof for thy Belovèd.   Lamb of God,

Thy blood redeemed the Nations, while I trode

The garden of thy gospel, bearing thence

Strange flowers of Love and holy Innocence,

And setting up aloft for all to see

Thy Hûleh-lilies, Faith, Hope, Charity ;

And of these three I knew the last was best

Because, like thee, dear Lord, 'twas lowliest !

Thy Witnesses ?   Countless as desert sands

Their bones are scatter'd o'er the seas and lands !

Whenc'er the Lamp of Life hath sunken low,

Whene'er Death beckon'd and 'twas time to go,

Where'er dark Pestilence and Disease had crawl'd,

Where'er the Soul was darken'd and appal'd,

Where mothers wept above their dead first-born,

Where children to green graves brought gifts forlorn

Of flowers and tears, where, struck 'spite helm and shield,

Pale warriors moan'd upon the battlefield,

Where Horror thicken'd as a spider's mesh

Round plague-smit men and lepers foul of flesh,

Where Love and Innocence were brought to shame,

And Life forgot its conscience and its aim,

Thy blessing, even as Light from far away,

Came bright and radiant upon eyes of clay

And turn'd the tears of pain to tears of bliss !

Nay, more, to Death itself thy loving kiss

Brought consecration ; he, that Angel sad,

Ran like a Lamb beside thee, and was glad

Uplooking in thy face ! '

He ceased, and lo !

Like warriors gathering when the trumpets blow,

Shapes of dead Saints arose, a shining throng,

And standing in their shrouds upraised the song

' Hosannah to the Lord ! '—Faint was the cry

Withering on the wind as if to die,

And loud as clarion-winds above the sound

Shrill'd the fierce anger of the hosts around ;

And while before the Storm his head was bowed

They rose like ocean waves and clamour'd aloud

For judgment on the Jew !

XVI

FAR as the sight
Could penetrate the blackness of the Night,
Stretchèd the multitudinous living Sea,
The angry waters of Humanity,
And lo! their voice was as the ocean's roar
Thund'rously beating on some sleepless shore ;
And he, the Man Divine, whose eyes were dim
With shining down on those who worshipt him,
Seem'd as a lonely pharos on a rock,
Firm in its place, yet shaken by the shock,
And ever blinded by the pitiless foam
Of waves that surge and thunder as they come !

And as I have seen, on some lone ocean-isle
Where never Summer lights or flowers may smile,

But where the fury of the Tempest blows,

The ocean birds in black and shivering rows

Huddle along the rocks; now one, alone,

Plunges upon the whirlwind, and is blown

Hither and thither as a straw, and then

Struggles back feebly to his rocky den,

There still to shiver and eye the dreadful flood

And with his comrades hungering for food

Ruffle the feathery crest and brood in fear :—

Ev'n so, those lonely Saints, who gather'd near

The Man forlorn, seem'd to the Sea of Life

Which rose around with ceaseless stress and strife,

And ever one of these, as if to face

The angry blast, would flutter from his place,

And driven hither and thither be backward blown,

And fall again with faint despairing moan

At his sad Master's feet !

                        Then as the Storm

Raged ever louder round his lonely form,

The Jew uplifted hands and cried aloud!

And in a moment, Darkness like a cloud
Cover'd him, the great whirlwinds ceased to roar,
And all those Waves of Life were still once more.

XVII

THEN said that Form who sat in Judgment there :

' Ye saw a mirage and ye thought it fair,

He brought a gospel and ye found it sweet,

Yea, deemed it heavenly manna and did eat,

Yet were ye empty still and never fed.

This man has given ye husks to eat, not bread.

He said " There is no Death ! " yet Death doth reign.

He promised you a gift no man may gain,

Yea, Life that shall endure eternally,

And told ye of a God no eye shall see,

Because He is not !　Bid him lift his hand

And show the Life Divine and Heavenly Land,

Bid him arise and take his Throne and reign !

He cannot, for he knoweth he dream'd in vain,

And empty of his hope he stands at last,

Now the full measure of his power hath passed.

Not yours the sin, poor Shadows of the Dead,

Not yours the shame, which rests upon his head

As dust and ashes.   Back to your graves, and sleep !

We judge the Shepherd, not the blameless sheep

Who gather'd on the heights to hear his voice

Cry down to deep on deep "Rejoice ! rejoice ! "

Fringe of his raiment that is riven and rent,

Breath of his nostrils that is lost and spent,

Thin echoes of his voice from out the tomb,

Go by.   This Man is ours, to judge and doom.'

He spake ; and quietly, without a word,

The Christ bow'd down his head, but those who heard,

His remnant, wringing hands and making moan,

Cried : ' Lord, thou hearest ?   Speak—and take thy
     Throne !

Still these wild waters of Humanity,

Walking thereon, as once on Galilee !

Our graves lie open yonder, but we are fain
To wake with thee and never to sleep again—
Unfold Thy Heavens, and bid these clouds give place,
That we may look upon the Father's face ! '

And Jesus answer'd not, but shook and wept.

Then the grey Mother to his bosom crept,
And with her thin hands touch'd his sad grey hair,
Saying ' My Son, my First-born !   Let me share
Thy failure or Thy glory !   Free or bound,
Cast down into the dust or throned and crown'd,
Thou art still my Son ! ' and kneeling at his feet,
That other Mary, gazing up to meet
The blessing of his eyes, cried ' Holy be
Thy Name, for all the joy it brought to me !
Not for thy Godhead did I hold thee dear,
Not for thy Father, who hath left thee here
Helpless, unpitied, homeless 'neath the skies,
But for the human love within thine eyes !

And wheresoe'er thou goest, howsoe'er

Thou fallest, tho' it be to Hell's despair,

I, thy poor handmaid, still would follow thee,

For in thy face is Love's Eternity,

And tho' thou art of all the World bereaven,

Still, where thou art, Belovèd, there is Heaven ! '

As some white Alpine peak, wrapt round with cloud,

Suddenly sweeps aside its clinging shroud

Of gloomy mists and vapours dark and chill,

And shines in lonely splendour clear and still,

With gleams of stainless ice and snow thrice shriven,

Against the azure of the opening Heaven,

So that the soul is shaken unaware

With that new glory desolately fair,—

E'en so the Christ, uprising suddenly

To loneliness of lofty sovereignty,

Cast off the darkness of despair and tower'd

High o'er the shadows that beneath him cower'd !

Then all was hush'd, while on his hoary head

Light from a million spheres was softly shed,

Fire from a million worlds that lit the Night

Fell on his face miraculously bright,

And even that Judge who watch'd him from afar

Seem'd but a storm-cloud shrinking 'neath a Star !

And thus, while heavenly anger lit his cheek

As still sheet-lightning lights the snowy peak,

He answered:

     ' Woe ! eternal Woe ! be yours

Who scorn the Eternal Pity which endures

While all things else pass by !   Your lips did thirst—

I brought ye water from the Founts which burst

Beneath the bright tread of my Father's feet !

Ye hunger'd, and I brought ye food to eat—

Manna, not husks or ashes : these ye chose,

And me, the living Christ, ye bruised with blows

And would have slain once more, and evermore !

Ye revell'd, and I moan'd without your door

Outcast and cold ; ye sinnèd in my Name,

And flung me then the raiment of your shame ;

Ye turn'd the heart of the Eternal One

'Gainst you, his children, and 'gainst me, his Son,

So that my promise grew a dream forlorn,

And all I sow'd in love, ye reapt in scorn.

Woe to ye all! and endless Woe to Me

Who deem'd that I could save Humanity!

The Father knew men better when He sent

His angel Death to be his instrument

And smite them ever down as with a sword!

Instead of Death, I offer'd ye my Word,

My Light, my Truth, my Life!—I wasted breath,

For though I gave ye these, ye turn'd to Death!

And I, your Lord, for love of you, denied

My Soul the sleep it sought, and rose to guide

Your footsteps to the Land we ne'er shall gain,

Because at last I know my Dream was vain!

I plough'd the rocks, and cast in rifts of stone

The seeds of Life Divine that ne'er have grown ;

I labour'd and I labour, last and first,

Within a barren Vineyard God hath curst ;

And now the Winter of mine age is here,

And one by one like leaves ye disappear,

While I, a blighted Tree, abide to show

The Woe of all Mankind, the eternal Woe

Which I, your Lord, must share ! '

                    Even so he spake,

Pallid in wrath ; but as low murmurs wake

Under the region of the Peak, and rise

To thunders answered from the thund'ring skies,

While cataract cries to cataract, and o'erhead

Heaven darkens into anger deep and dread,

Cries from the shadowy legions answer'd him,

Wild voices wail'd, and all the Void grew dim

With cloud on cloud.   So that serene sad Face

Was blotted out of vision for a space,

And out of darkness on that radiant form

Sprang the fierce pards and panthers of the Storm !

Then the Earth trembled, and the crimson levin

Shot swift and lurid o'er the vaults of Heaven,

And thunder answer'd thunder with crash on crash

As beast doth beast, but at each lightning-flash

I saw him standing pale and terrible,

Unscath'd yet swathen as with fire from Hell!

But lo, from out the darkness round his feet

There came a voice most passionately sweet

Crying 'Adonai! Lord! Forgive us, even

Altho' our sins be seventy times seven!

Comfort the remnant of thy flock, and bless

Thy Well Belovèd!'—and my Soul could guess

Whose voice had call'd, for at the voice's sound

He trembled and he reach'd towards the ground

With eager trembling hands; and at the touch

Of her who had loved not wisely, but too much,

His force fell from him, and he wept aloud,

While heavily his hoary head was bowed

In utter impotence of Deity!

·

XVIII

EVEN then, methought, that angry living Sea
Surged round him, and again I did discern
The Phantoms of Golgotha !—Soldiers stern
Who pointed with their spears and pricked him on,
While on his shoulders drooping woe-begone
They thrust the great black Cross !   Upon his head
A crown of thorns was set, and dript its red
Dark drops upon his brow, while loud they cried
' Lo, this is Jesus whom we crucified,
And lo, he hath risen, and shall die once more ! '
And as a waif is cast on some dark shore
By breaking waves of Ocean and is ta'en
Back by the surge again and yet again,
Even so the Man was tost, till he lay prone,
Breathless, a ragged heap, beneath the Throne.

Golgotha! Like the very Hill of Death,

Skull-shapen, yet a living thing of breath,

The dark Judge loom'd, with orbs of fateful flame,

And motion'd back the crying crowd that came

Shrieking for judgment on that holy head ;

And lo, they faltered back !

                    Then the Voice said :

' Arise, O Jew ! '

             And Jesus rose.

                        ' Again

Take up thy Cross ! '

                 Calm, with no moan of pain,

Jesus took up the Cross. While 'neath its load

He shook as if to fall, his white hair snow'd

Around his woeful face and wistful eyes !

While thus he stood, bowed down in pain, the cries

Of those who loved him pierced his suffering heart.

Trembling he heard again, with lips apart

And listening eyes, the faithful remnant moan :

'Adonai !   Lord and Master !   Take thy Throne,

And claim thy Kingdom !' but with clamorous sound

Of laughter fierce and mad the cry was drowned,

And at his naked breast the forkèd light

Stabb'd like a knife, while thro' the gulfs of Night

The thunders roar'd !

                   Trembling at last he rose,

And as a wind-smit tree shakes off the snows

That cling upon its boughs, he gatherèd

His strength together, and with lifted head

Gazed at his Judge ; and lo, again the storm

Of darkness ebbed away and left his Form

Serene and luminous as an Alpine peak

Shining above these valleys !   On his cheek

The sheeted light gleam'd softly, while on high

The silent azure open'd like an eye

And gazed upon him, pitilessly fair.

So round about him as he waited there

Silence like starlight fell, till suddenly,

Like surge innumerable of one great Sea,

A million voices moaned, ' Speak now his Doom ! '

XIX

Then, pointing with dark finger thro' the gloom
On him who stood erect with hoary head,
The Judge gazed down with dreadful eyes, and said:

' Ere yet I speak thy Doom that must be spoken
Before the World whose great heart thou hast broken,
Hast thou another word to say, O Jew?'

And the Jew answer'd, while the heavenly blue
Fill'd like an eye with starry crystal tears,
' Far have I wander'd thro' the sleepless years—
Be pitiful, O Judge, and let me die!'

' Death to him, Death!' I heard the voices cry
Of that great Multitude.   But the Voice said:

'Nay!

Death that brought peace thyself didst seek to slay !

Death that was merciful and very fair,

Sweet dove-eyed Death that hush'd the Earth's despair,

Death that shed balm on tirèd eyes like thine,

Death that was Lord of Life and all Divine,

Thou didst deny us, offering instead

The Soul's fierce famine that can ne'er be fed—

Death shall abide to bless all things that be,

But evermore shall turn aside from thee—

Hear then thy Doom !'

He paused, while all around

The Sea of Life lay still without a sound,

And on the Man Divine, Death's King and Lord,

The sacrament of heavenly Light was pour'd.

'Since thou hast quicken'd what thou canst not kill,

Awaken'd famine thou canst never still,

Spoken in madness, prophesied in vain,

And promised what no thing of clay shall gain,

Thou shalt abide while all things ebb and flow,

Wake while the weary sleep, wait while they go,

And treading paths no human feet have trod

Search on still vainly for thy Father, God;

Thy blessing shall pursue thee as a curse

To hunt thee, homeless, thro' the Universe;

No hand shall slay thee, for no hand shall dare

To strike the godhead Death itself must spare!

With all the woes of Earth upon thy head,

Uplift thy Cross, and go.   Thy Doom is said.'

XX

AND lo ! while all men come and pass away,

That Phantom of the Christ, forlorn and grey,

Haunteth the Earth with desolate footfall. . . .

God help the Christ, that Christ may help us all !